Northwest Fusion

A Collection of Stories, Plays, Essays
and one really quirky Poem.

by

Bill Branley

One Sock Press

Seattle, Washington

ISBN-10: 0977856135
ISBN-13: 978-0-9778561-3-8

DEDICATION

This collection is dedicated to the many Pacific Northwest writers who have inspired me. I came here with the South in me, and it's still there, but with moss growing over it.

CONTENTS

ANGELA

"The what?" David looked at his wife.

"Doula. D-O-U-L-A," Angela said. "Where have you been for the past nine months?"

He paused. This was a time to be agreeable and non-critical, which meant not pointing out that she had said 'doula' with a mouthful of food. "Sorry. I just didn't catch what you had said."

"Oh, oh, oh!" Angela laid one hand on her stomach and with the other she gripped the dining room table.

"Another contraction?" asked David.

She nodded, with her eyes closed. He could see pain in her face, and felt a churning in his own gut. With each contraction, his anxiety increased. He felt this way when large, life-changing events loomed ahead. And he knew this one was close: he fully expected that on this night their second child was going to be born.

"Should we call the doula?"

She exhaled. "Not yet."

The doula was a labor coach. This was different from a midwife, he had learned. The doula wasn't going to deliver the baby: she was going to help Angela through labor. The midwife would deliver the baby. He hadn't known that childbirthing had become so compartmentalized.

Angela looked at him with a determined expression. "She said to call when contractions are ten minutes apart." Even at forty weeks pregnant, she was beautiful. Dark curls framed her flushed face and emphasized her deep brown eyes. She had given up her family name of Tortorich, which went so perfectly with her looks, in order to take his totally ordinary name of Smith. Angela Smith. She had made other sacrifices, too. Their first child was born after four days of labor followed by a Cesarean. When she got pregnant again she made a vow to do it differently.

1

"Trust me, I know what you want," he said. "A totally natural childbirth. No drugs, no c-section. You want that baby to slide out like a fish."

"David, fish metaphors should not be used with a person who doesn't like seafood." Pause. "Oh my."

"Another? That was quick!"

"No, that was a kick. Wow, he's a strong one."

"How do you know it's a he? You said you didn't want to know."

"I don't really know, I just feel it. He's kicking the way Tony kicked."

Tony was their first child, now three and having a sleepover at a neighbor's house.

"I'm still hoping for a girl," he said.

She reached over and laid her warm, puffy fingers on his arm. She was a walking bag of blood and emotions. "I just want it to come out."

"Tonight," said David. "It's going to be tonight. I'm ready."

"Oh that's good to know. The husband is ready. Thank God. Let's have the baby." Angela got up from the table and carefully balanced herself before taking a step. "It's time for another walk."

They went out into a June evening. As David debated whether to lock the house, the screen door slipped from his fingers and closed with a whack.

Angela froze. "David, you know I can't stand the sound of that door slamming."

"It slipped. I was checking for my keys."

"You don't need to lock it. We're only going around the block."

They reached the street. Angela raised her face to the last of the day's light and sniffed the air. The sun was down, but traces of color lingered. Clouds formed in the south, and a pair of tall swaying birch trees caught the sun's rays with upturned leaves.

"It's going to rain," said David.

"Rain would feel good," said Angela. "The plants need it. My asparagus is drying up."

"But didn't you say the baby kicked whenever you ate asparagus?" asked David.

"But one day he'll be out, and I can eat asparagus again."

"Ouch." She looked like she was going to collapse. David held her shoulders; they were warm. Her whole body was a warm bath with a baby in it. She was a steam engine, idling, waiting to be called to service. He had read that a pregnant woman lying on a sofa burns more calories than a thirty-year-old man walking up a hill. He could feel concentrated energy radiating from her body, mingling with the evening heat.

"That was a doozy," she said.

"Maybe we should go back."

She looked at her watch. "They're getting close enough. Call the doula."

He whipped out his cell phone. At last, he had something to do.

Her name was Victoria. Twenty minutes and two contractions later, she swept past David into the house, leaving in her wake a whiff of incense and perfume mixed with moist summer air. David felt the swish of her long, flowing skirt and heard the creak of sturdy sandals. The doula had arrived. With hardly a handshake and a how-do-you-do, she asked David to put a kettle of water on for tea and then disappeared into the bedroom, where Angela waited.

David read the business section of the paper while the electric kettle slowly warmed and rattled and began to emit steam.

He poked his head into the bedroom. Candles glowed from the nightstand, the dresser, and a small footstool by the window. They gave off an unfamiliar scent: sweet, like lilies. "Water's almost hot. What kind of tea would you like?"

"Oh thank you, David," said Angela, sitting up in bed, leaning against a wedge of pillows. Even in the dim light he could see that her face was brighter and more relaxed. She was now in the doula's hands.

"I brought some herbal tea for stress reduction," said Victoria, handing David two tea bags. "We both need it. Would you like a cup, too?"

"No, thanks. I'm going to have coffee."

"Hmm," she said.

When he returned with the tea, Angela's shirt was pulled up over her belly. Victoria pressed gently on the sides and bottom of the bulge. They studied it with a look of wonder. Backlit by candlelight, Angela's stomach reminded David of a basketball. Her face, in profile, was a series of curves from forehead to chin. The light emphasized the new puffiness that had come into her face in the last few weeks. She was looking more like a baby even as she was about to have one.

"The head's right here," said Victoria. She guided Angela's fingers to a place low on the abdomen.

Angela looked at David as she patted the spot like she was comforting a child. "I feel him," she said, then winced as another contraction seized her. David wondered if Victoria was timing the contractions.

"I brought tea," said David. He stood there, waiting for someone to shoo him away.

Victoria took both mugs and handed one to Angela, who raised it to her mouth and drew in the hot beverage with extended lips. The steam rose and mingled with the curls of her hair.

"How do you feel?" David asked.

"Much better."

"Great. When do we go to the hospital?"

"Not for a while," said Victoria. "We want to do as much of the labor at home as we can."

Later they went for another walk. The rain had come and gone, leaving fat droplets of water on the grass. It was the kind of summer night David liked. Looking down the street, he saw steam rising from wet pavement into the glow of the street lamps. The illumination was softened by the moist air, as though a filter had been applied. It was not a real street scene, but a painting of one.

"Oh," exclaimed Angela, holding her stomach. Her 'Ohs' were not short, but long and drawn out, like a moan or a hum or just a syllable.

He stopped in the middle of the street while she rested a hand on his shoulder and took several deep, controlled breaths of air. It occurred to David that his thoughts and Angela's had been worlds apart. She was not gazing at the summer scene before them and dreaming of how it looked. No, every inch of her being was focused on the task at hand.

"Victoria says they'll get worse. I can't imagine it," she said, almost crying.

"Angela, you're doing great so far. I'm really proud of you."

"By this time, with Tony, I was already on pain relievers," she said.

"I don't remember that detail," he said.

"I remember every detail. Only now do I appreciate what the pain relievers were doing."

"You mean, how much pain was being relieved?"

She chuckled. "Don't make me laugh. I would love to laugh right now, but it hurts." She looked at him. Now she was all love and affection. "But I can hear that humor in your voice. I love you."

"I love you, too. We're doing this together, okay? I'm right here, sharing the pain with you."

"That's a nice thought. Imagine if you could share pain, if you could feel a portion of someone's pain so they would feel less of it, like maybe half."

"Or maybe fifty-five percent. You would need a pain meter."

"Ooh, ooh." She cradled her stomach. "I told you not to make me laugh. You just gave me a contraction."

"Good, I'm helping."

"Let's go back. I'm ready for another cup of tea."

At midnight, David paced the living room floor. He couldn't read or sleep. Ten minutes ago, a painful shriek from the bedroom made him cringe. He imagined important body parts moving, shifting, widening, making way. It rattled his nerves to think of something as large as a baby inside of an adult body.

He heard his name called from the bedroom. He rushed in; craving a duty to perform, anything.

Victoria handed him a bowl with a damp washcloth in it. "Could you freshen that up with cool water? And I need another with warm water."

"Two washcloths, one cool, one hot," David replied, with a voice he

4

had used as a short-order cook during his college years. Angela had been a regular customer at the diner. She liked the way he echoed orders called out by the waitress.

"And could I get a glass of water with that?" asked Victoria, picking up the routine with ease.

"Yes, ma'am," said David. She was quick. He looked at Angela, who smiled weakly from her perch against the pillows. "Can I get you anything?" he asked.

"A baby," she said.

David rushed out of the room. The old washcloth smelled of perspiration: Angela's. She was having an all-night workout. It made his occasional morning jog around the neighborhood seem like napping by comparison. He returned with the clean washcloths and handed them to Victoria.

"You can help," said Victoria, handing him a cloth. "The cool one is for her cheeks and forehead."

David knelt on the bed and gently pressed the cool cloth against Angela's forehead. He saw immediate relief in her face. Meanwhile, Victoria applied the warm cloth to Angela's legs and stomach and abdomen for the purpose, she explained, of relaxing the muscles and tissue around the cervix. "We have to let them stretch, you see." No, he didn't see how it was mechanically possible, but there was no turning back from this voyage.

Angela lurched and cried out. "Wow," she said. "This baby is awesome."

"Awesome?" said David. "That's not the word I expected you to use."

She gripped his hand. "Just relax, David. Everything'll be fine."

It took a moment for her words to sink in: she's the one having her insides rearranged to a new shape, and she's telling me to relax.

CONVALESCENCE

I met Juanita in the day room. That was where the nurses took me to watch television and play games. It was kind of bland, with bad art on the walls, but it had good light. There was a ping pong table, which I thought was a cruel joke: I figured it would be a long time before I played ping pong.

At first the nurses would wheel me down there and prop me in front of the television and hand me a remote control. Then they let me go on my own once I learned the way. One day a nurse wheeled in a woman with dark hair and a scowl on her face and left her parked next to me. After the nurse left I offered my new companion the remote control and she used it to turn off the television.

"My father called it the idiot box," she said.

"My name is Louis," I said, opting not to challenge her on the issue of the television, guessing I would probably lose anyway.

"I am Juanita. How do you do?" she said, with tired politeness.

I shrugged. "I lost my left leg and I feel like shit. How about you?"

She shrugged back. "I lost my left arm and I hate myself."

"Do you want to play ping pong?" I asked.

She looked at me like I had just asked her to have sex on the floor. Then she laughed. I realized she was pretty. "You will have the advantage, since you have two arms."

"But you have two legs. You can maneuver," I said.

"You're serious?"

"C'mon. Just try it."

A moment earlier I hadn't thought I would ever play ping pong again, and now I was about to face a one-armed contestant. It fit my mood: angry, mean. I had a need to beat somebody at something. I wheeled over to the table. Because she was an arm amputee she had a powered wheel chair. I

6

heard the whir of a motor as she buzzed over. The two paddles and the ball were lying on a side table. I handed a blue paddle to her.

"I want the red one," she said.

I gave her the red one. I don't think she really cared; she just wanted to make a demand. I understood perfectly. That's what happens when you become an amputee.

I went to the far end. "Ready?" I asked.

She rolled her eyes. "Whatever." She was prettier when she smiled.

Thinking I should start easy with her, I bounced the ball and tapped it gently to the other side. She slammed it back at an angle that sent it whizzing by my outstretched arm.

"You've, um, played before," I observed.

"I played a lot of ping pong with my brothers in Puerto Rico when they were out of work, which was most of the time."

"I see."

I retrieved the ball and served it to her again, this time determined to show her that a two-armed person can beat a one-armed person at anything. But it was hopeless. Juanita was so good that I could not have beat her with three arms against her one.

"More?" she asked.

"No thanks. I'm humiliated enough." Fortunately the nurse returned and ordered us back upstairs for dinner.

Juanita waved and smiled as she was escorted away. Damn she was pretty.

The next day I asked her when she got her injury.

"September 24th," she said.

"Wow. That's the same day I got hit. Roadside bomb?"

She nodded. "Anbar Province."

"My bomb was in Baghdad." I didn't have to ask for more details. I could guess what she went through. When we hit our bomb my ears felt crushed by the loudest noise I have ever heard, even on the artillery range. Then there was the sound of stuff ripping and something crawling up my leg, like bugs. People screamed and I heard voices shouting from the radio. My memory is hazy after that. I was transported somewhere. Later I woke up in a surgical unit. There was a stump where my left leg had been. The very first image to enter my mind was that of my wife and two sons back at Fort Benning, Georgia. Dad now has one leg. Dad the baseball coach and marathon runner. That Dad. Strong, healthy. It was the last thing I expected to happen in Iraq. I figured I would come back alive or dead. Not crippled. After the surgical unit I was flown here, a military hospital in Germany, for a period of convalescence. This was meant to prepare me for my return to the States and my family. I received physical therapy and counseling and learned about my options for artificial limbs. Turns out there's quite a lot you can do with an artificial leg. I talked to my wife and sons by video hookup, but they only saw my upper body. They knew what happened because I told them, but the reality would not sink in until they saw me in person. I dreaded that moment more than anything in the world. I imagined the looks on their faces and it drove me crazy.

I realized Juanita was looking at me silently, waiting for my thoughts to return to the present moment. I figured she knew my thoughts without having to ask. "Are you married?" I asked her.

"Husband and two kids in Virginia," she said. "You see, I am a Reservist. Now I get to go home and be a one-arm soccer Mom in the suburbs, and join the other Moms in their Volvos and SUVs, holding their babies in one arm and their lattes in the other."

The scowl had returned to her face, the one I saw the first time we met. She was close to tears. When you become an amputee there's a fear that your loved ones will never really feel the same way about you. Regardless of how kind they are and how patient and loving they are. You are not a whole person anymore, and you are certain they love you just a little bit less.

"Would you like to play cards?" I asked.

She looked at me through her scowl and smiled just a tiny bit. "I want to beat you in ping pong again."

"Figures," I said. But I liked her attitude.

We started to volley and I saw an opening that would allow me to slam a shot toward the corner of the table. The ball careened off the walls and bounced on the floor. It made her angry.

"I'll get it," I said.

"No, I can get it," she said.

We both headed for the ball. The wheel of her chair caught it and sent it spinning away. I steered to catch it. She cut me off and tried to step on the ball with her foot, but managed to knock it against the wall. She laughed brightly. It had turned into a game. The ball ricocheted in my direction. I was determined to steer my chair with my arms and use my good leg to catch the ball. I stomped at it wildly. She laughed at my efforts. The prettiness returned to her face. Finally I trapped it and leaned over to retrieve the elusive ping pong ball. She could not stop laughing.

I presented it to her gallantly. "The ball, your ladyship," I said.

She took the ball, and my hand, in her right hand. Her touch was electrifying. Without thinking, I brought my other hand to hers and held it. Her eyes were all warmth and affection now. And then the miracle occurred: I became aware of a sensation that I thought had disappeared from my life forever. I was so surprised I had to look down at myself. And there it was: a state of arousal that threatened to break the seams of my pajamas.

Suddenly, with embarrassment, I realized I was staring at my own erection and Juanita was staring at it with me. "I'm sorry, I, uh..., you see it's been such a long time...I haven't, uh..." I quickly pulled my robe over the pup tent that had formed in my lap.

"Don't worry about it," she said. Now the softness of her voice matched her skin and her eyes.

I took a deep breath. "Do you still want to play ping pong?"

"I think it's time for lunch," she said.

"Good idea."

Juanita and I lived on the same floor of the same wing, with a dozen other amputees. I had a three-person room, but the other two beds were empty. After lights-out you were supposed to stay in your room, but once you got to know the routine of the nursing staff you could ignore the rules a bit. Sometimes patients needed to walk around at night because they couldn't sleep.

Juanita came into my room at eleven o'clock. That was right after the nurses went to a reduced schedule and the halls were dark. I had been thinking of her, and my erection, all day. It had probably been six months since I felt that hard. There's something about the stress of a war zone, especially Iraq with those fucking IEDs, and knowing any day could be your last. Then there was the bomb with my name on it, which I assumed had killed off whatever potential for sex had still existed in me. It was another reason I was apprehensive about going home. How do I say to my wife, 'Honey, not only do I have one leg, but, as a bonus, I can't have sex any more.'

She entered on foot. In fact, Juanita was able to walk fine, but the nurses made her use a wheel chair because they didn't want her to fall and not be able to catch herself.

She entered my curtained bedchamber like a spirit, a fantasy come true. I turned my face to her and whispered, "Hello." With her good arm she pushed her pajamas and underwear to the floor and stepped out of them. It took nothing more than the sight of her nakedness for my erection to return with a vengeance. I pushed the covers away. She lifted the elastic band of my pajamas and helped me push them over my one-point-two legs. The cool air only heightened my arousal. She gripped me gently and I had to clench my teeth to keep from shouting with pleasure. She unbuttoned her pajama top and let it fall to the floor. Juanita was amazingly capable for a person with one arm.

She stepped on the rail of my bed and was about to climb in when it hit me: wait a minute, I'm married. She sensed my hesitation, even though I said nothing and made no obvious gesture. Yet, something real had ballooned between our panting bodies.

"What is it?" she asked, pausing over me, her breasts so close I could have licked them.

9

"Listen," I whispered, "you are absolutely gorgeous, and I'm horny as hell, but I'm also married. I don't know if I really want to do this."

She looked at me for several seconds but I could read the expression on her face. The heat we had generated began to dissipate as though a breeze had blown past us. She stepped down to the floor and quickly pulled her pajamas back on. For a moment I couldn't believe I blew such an amazing opportunity. What has happened to me? I watched with sadness as a patch of smooth skin on her hips was covered with wrinkled cotton cloth.

Then she said, "You are so right. It was a stupid idea." She turned and left.

I dressed myself and let my head fall to the pillow. The room was lonelier and colder than it had been.

I didn't see Juanita for two days, mainly because I read a book and the newspapers in my room, and I had physical therapy classes. I knew I was avoiding her. At the same time, I felt as though I had saved my marriage.

During those days I had several phone calls with my wife and sons. It was fun hearing about home and we talked about things we were going to do, but I had to keep reminding them about my wheelchair. My wife was nervous about that, about my new body shape. I could hear it in her voice, and my feelings of inadequacy returned. I couldn't blame her: she marries a guy who's perfectly healthy and now he has one leg. Once again I had the sense that it wasn't going to be the same, that she was going to love me a little bit less.

After a couple of days I missed Juanita's company so I went down to the day room when I thought she would be there. I found her reading by a window. I wheeled next to her and she looked up and smiled. There were several other people in the room, playing ping pong and watching television.

I touched the back of her hand with my fingers and once again felt her warmth. It was like a drug. "I hope you aren't mad at me," I said.

"I assumed you were angry with me," she said.

"Not at all. In fact, I'm curious to know what your idea was. Why did you say 'it was a stupid idea.'?"

She looked around the room. "We can't talk here. Can I come see you tonight?" She added quickly, "just to talk."

I laughed. "Sure." Then I pulled out my book. "Do you mind if I sit by the window here and read with you?"

"I would love that."

We read until dinner time and then returned to our rooms. The hands of my clock moved maddeningly slow through the evening hours. I tried to read but couldn't. A series of images flowed through my head: Juanita naked, my wife, Juanita's breasts, my wife, Juanita's dark pubic hair against her light brown skin, my wife.

The nurses changed shifts and made rounds. The hallway lights dimmed. Juanita stepped through my curtain at eleven-thirty. I rested my hand on her waist. She leaned over and kissed me.

"I missed you," she said.

"I want to hear your stupid idea," I said.

In what seemed like seconds her pajama bottoms and underwear were on the floor and my body's response was so instantaneous I thought I heard cotton threads tearing below the covers. I flung the covers off and frantically pushed my own pajamas around my stump. She removed her top and climbed over me, but this time nothing came between us.

"My stupid idea was to practice having sex," she said after she had arranged her naked body next to mine. She teased my erection with her fingers. There was something about her touch that drove me wild.

"Practice?" I said. "Since when do humans need to practice."

"Typical male attitude," she said. "You know there is an art to this."

"Can I be your student?"

Then her face was serious. "You see, I am very worried about my husband accepting me when I return home. I have to know that, even with one arm, I can be sexy."

I didn't have time to ponder this because apparently the talking was over. With her good arm she pushed herself up. Her body was so gorgeous I hardly noticed her stump. And she seemed to pay no attention to mine. The contrast was striking: mine was a severed thigh, large, like a cut from a fallen tree. Her stump had once been a firm and shapely arm. Now it protruded from her shoulder like a third breast. I didn't have much time to dwell on this, because she was on a mission, and she went about it like an infantry squad on patrol. We explored each other's bodies for several excruciating minutes. I slid a finger between her legs and found it warm and wet.

She giggled. "This oven's been preheated for hours," she said.

She climbed on top of me and we discovered that our stumps left us feeling strangely off-balance. However, I found that if I put one foot on the floor, while lying on my back, I had better control. She used her one arm to prop herself over me, and I supported her waist with my two hands. I lowered her gently onto me while she struggled to contain her voice. I had the feeling she was ordinarily a screamer.

I think it was the best ninety seconds of my life. The need to keep quiet made it almost unbearable, but we peaked noiselessly before collapsing into a sweaty heap of partial limbs and bandages. We said nothing for several moments. There were no questions, no discussion, no analysis. We simply savored the most exquisite moment of our lives. And as we lay there, with our breathing subsiding to a normal tempo, I realized that I still had one foot firmly planted on the floor. A foot in reality, and the rest of me in heaven.

She left the room as she had come in, dissolving through the curtains like an apparition. I wondered for a moment whether it had been a dream. But I knew by the limpness I now felt that it was real. I realized then, as I lay alone, still savoring her scent and the feel of her hair and skin, that it was human contact that I had been craving. I suspected that we both needed to expose ourselves, stumps and all, to another human besides a medical professional and have that other human accept us without condition. It was a test, and we both passed. I understood her stupid idea, which was not so stupid.

Of course, we tested that theory a dozen times over the next several weeks. After all, one wants to get these things right. Juanita brought oil and we massaged each other. We experimented with different positions. I got good at having sex with one-point-two legs and it motivated me to pay more attention to my artificial limbs briefings.

I am now at the end of my convalescent stay in Germany. Juanita left a few days ago. Myself and several others are scheduled to fly tomorrow to Dover Air Force Base, in Delaware, where our families will meet us. That's where the initial greeting will take place. That's where my wife and sons will see me in all my glory for the first time. But now I am ready.

Juanita visited me one final time to say good-bye. She made her stealthy entrance at eleven-thirty, but did not push her pajamas to the floor. My body by that point had been conditioned to respond like a salivating dog. She looked sympathetically at my erection and gave it a little squeeze.

"I came to say good-bye, to you and your friend," she said.

"What?" I must have looked like a little boy who has just been denied an ice cream cone.

She giggled. "It's time to end our little romance. But you have helped me in a way that all of the therapists and trainers and counselors could not have. You have reminded me that I am still a healthy woman and I can be a sexy wife to my husband. I am strong now. Thanks to you."

I realized she was right, of course, even though it meant we would not have one last roll in the hospital bed as I had fantasized about all day. On the other hand, I knew that I, too, had the confidence to go home to my wife without my leg and say, 'but look at the bright side, honey: I can have some damn good sex.'

I held Juanita's hand. "I thought greeting my family was going to be hard. This is even harder."

She kissed me. "Good bye. I love you," she said.

Now I stare at the ceiling, elated, nervous. I loved Juanita, but I know now that I am still in love with my wife. It's all a question of confidence. "If I am confident, she will be okay with my new limitations. Yet, my stomach is rattling with excitement. I feel like I am going to float away, but I know what to do about that. I put one foot on the floor.

SHOPPING AT MAISON BLANCHE

Miss Marie waited in the front yard for Gerard. There was no shade, so she spread her lace handkerchief over her eyes to get some relief from the sun. It was a fierce heat that had built up gradually, starting the day after the storm with ghostly columns of steam rising from every surface. Then the streets dried, the mud cracked up like pieces of a puzzle, and the yard turned to a fine powder that formed little clouds in the air at the slightest movement. Even by Louisiana standards it was hot; she couldn't remember it ever being so hot. She carefully adjusted the white handkerchief so it covered her face. The filtered light came through and backlit her initials, M.P., for Marie Patine, embroidered into one corner in fancy script. She remembered getting the handkerchief, a gift for her First Communion sixty-two years ago. She rode the streetcar with her mother and shopped for the first time at Maison Blanche.

Where's that Gerard? She sighed. My, he was a difficult nephew. Before the storm he had the nerve to insist that she ride to Baton Rouge with him. Who ever heard of going all the way to Baton Rouge to sit out a hurricane?

"I was born in this house sixty-nine years ago and I haven't left for no storm and I don't intend to start," she had told him on the phone. He was the son of her sister, Camille, who had briefly been a nun and then fled the convent and had five kids. There was no escaping that sentence; the Lord had had plans for her from the start.

Marie struggled to keep herself awake. She thought if she could find just a little bit of water she would feel much better. She should have gone with Gerard. What an old fool I am! She touched the gash on her head. It was soft and frightening. They say you can only lose so much blood before you die; she wondered how much had already oozed from her head and dripped into the dirt.

Gerard had been right. The storm was the big one, the one they always said would come and wipe out the parish. From her bedroom window she saw the water rise up of the canal. It charged like soldiers out of a trench with guns drawn and spirit voices raised in a blood-curdling rebel yell. The angry army of water came straight for the house, foaming and hurling itself onward. Her massive oak wardrobe, which had rested over the same piece of floor for all of her sixty-nine years--which had been assembled on that spot and was so heavy that not even her grandfather and his two brothers and the egg man could move it--was lifted miraculously into the air and flung against the opposite wall, where it crashed and turned and came to rest. As it did so, one of the ornate, hand-carved corners of the wardrobe sank a half-inch into her temple. Water rushed up to her chest and as she fell back her blood mixed with the water and her leg was caught and it twisted and sent pain streaking up to her waist. She pulled the leg free in spite of the pain and tried to wade toward the kitchen, but the kitchen moved away from her: the house was splitting in two. The sturdy Cajun cottage, built by her grandfather to withstand a hundred hurricanes, the place where her mother was born, the place where Marie was born and the place she inherited when her mother died because her father was already dead and she was the one sister who never married and was the old spinster, although everyone knew she hated that word and would never use it around her, that place, was now coming apart at the seams. The big surge. Her uncle had described what would happen: "the surge'll come up the Mississippi River from the Gulf and will flow into every canal and every bayou and every little ditch and the water will be lifted right out like the hand of God come down and parted the seas." Then she fainted.

Just before fainting, Marie looked back into her bedroom and saw that the wardrobe door had flung open and her clothes floated out: a yellow Easter dress, a business suit that she wore when she worked as a receptionist at the power company, a black funeral dress that she wore to the funerals of her parents and grandparents and all of their siblings, who seemed to die off slowly at first but then went in a stampede. Then other clothes came out of the wardrobe, the old hand-me-downs that had belonged to her mother and grandmother and some of her aunts and her older sisters. An old-fashioned coat with fur around the collar seemed to swim out on its own, a hat with a long feather popped out of its box, a treasure trove of Maison Blanche handkerchiefs escaped from their moth-balled prison. Marie felt wet blackness closing in on her. She was sure that she was near death because she was imagining the most amazing things. She saw her Ma'mere, her grandmother, climb out of the wardrobe wearing a dress that Marie had not seen in many years. Ma'mere stood above the water and looked down, disapprovingly, at Marie, who was terrified and wanted to hide. Then her Aunt Magda, her mother's oldest sister, stuck her head through the opening and looked around as though peeking out of her coffin and her eyes came to rest on Marie, who was now collapsed in dirty water on the hallway floor. The storm water had barreled through her home like a crowd of rude visitors and now mingled with the water and mud beneath the raised, wooden house. All of this happened in a span of time that she could not measure, she only knew that as her eyes closed her dead relatives were looking at her with a very sad expression.

The water receded as quickly as it had come up. There was one pulverizing attack, followed by an immediate retreat that took with it trash cans, lumber, half the kitchen, the front door, the screen porch, the crepe myrtle by the porch, the pecan tree that was in the middle of the front yard, the garden fence that kept the nutria out, the two bicycles that Marie had not ridden in fifteen years, the lawnmower, the roof over the garage and the hose pipe that had rotted from disuse.

When Marie woke up she found herself on the concrete stoop that had led up to where there had been a kitchen door. Now the stoop was a little island in a sea of rubble. Some yards away from her, half of her home stood precariously upright, it's innards exposed like a doll house. Her cotton dress was soaked with blood and her leg was blue and useless. Aunt Magda and Ma'mere stood not far away, surveying the ruins. Then they saw her.

"Are you ready to go, Marie? You're always the last one ready," said Aunt Magda.

"Where are we going?"

"Dear child, have you not been paying attention? We're going to Maison Blanche, on Canal Street," said Ma'mere. "I still say it's the finest department store in New Orleans."

"I have nothing to wear," said Marie.

"Correcting that problem is the purpose of our trip," said Aunt Magda with her chin raised high.

"But I have no money," said Marie.

"You don't need money," said Ma'mere.

Marie stayed on the stoop for two days and watched the weather and the ground change from wet to dry and when it did she dragged herself to the spot in the front yard where the pecan tree had been. There was no sign of the tree. Even the fallen trunk was gone with the surge. She could see down her street and saw nothing but ruins where houses of her neighbors had been. She was sure that eventually Gerard would come for her. He would come back from Baton Rouge to check on her. If only she could hold out till then.

"Are you ready, dear?" said Ma'mere.

"Where to now?" asked Marie, feeling very weak and frightened. Ma'mere wore a splendid white dress that shone brilliantly in the sun. Marie had seen the dress in a photograph taken when Ma'mere was only eighteen. How could she still fit into that dress? It was very confusing.

Ma'mere and Magda shook their heads disapprovingly. "Some girls need a written invitation," said Magda.

"That's the younger gen'ration for you. Maison Blanche is going to close if you don't hurry, Marie. Now let's go."

Marie smiled and squinted at her grandmother. "I'm coming Ma'mere. I'm coming now."

"J"

It rained hard on the day Odile Boudreaux brought her newborn son home from the hospital. Her husband, August, held the umbrella as she stepped from the car with the blue bundle safely in her arms.

"The boy's got some lungs," said August, referring to the wailing that could be heard over the loud downpour.

"He needs changing," Odile said. With surprising agility she darted across the inch of standing water that had collected on the lawn and hurried through the door that August held open for her.

In the living room of the house, a dark-haired girl of two climbed down from the lap of a wrinkled woman sitting in a rocking chair. "Baby," Annette cried as she tried to catch a glimpse of her new baby brother, who had been named August, Jr.

"Lord, let poor Augie have a clean diaper first," said Odile.

Odile went to her bedroom and closed the door. She laid the red-faced baby on the bed, next to a stack of cloth diapers that had been washed and laid out. She removed the pins from his diaper and set them aside. Almost as soon as she took her hand away from the pins they began to vibrate. Odile looked at them, puzzled. Then, as Augie continued to express his discomfort, the pins rose about six inches off the bed and hung in the air, vibrating slightly.

Odile's eyes widened as she passed a trembling hand beneath the pins and above them. They were suspended in the air, as if by magic. She grabbed them in her fist and turned and looked at her baby with an expression of puzzlement mixed with worry.

+++++++

August Boudreaux parked his car in front of a small store with the

18

words Boudreaux's Hardware painted in block letters in the front window. The rear door of the car opened and a young boy wearing a New Orleans Saints tee-shirt jumped to the curb.

"Can I hammer something, Dad?" said Augie.

"Yes, Augie, but remember the deal we made: no funny business, no tricks, no stuff flying around the store. And if you do it in front of a customer we go home."

"Yes, Dad," said Augie with bowed head.

August took a long look at his son while he turned the keys in the dead bolt. "Your Mother has turned five shades of gray since you were born and I'm not doing much better myself."

"Yes, Dad."

The morning was uneventful. The Boudreauxs had learned that the way to handle their special son was to keep him calm, not get him excited. At the tender age of four he was getting better at controlling his bizarre ability to raise metal objects, apparently by merely thinking about them. But he had a long way to go: sometimes objects went up when he didn't consciously think about them.

By lunch time, Augie had managed to bend a long row of nails by trying to hammer them into a two-by-four, supposedly to make a hat rack. Everything seemed fine until Mrs. Dupre came in with her dog, Chief, a large German Shepherd.

Augie was very afraid of large dogs. When he looked up and saw that he was at eye-level with Chief he let out a shriek and about a hundred nails and screws flew up from their little trays and settled on the ceiling. Mrs. Dupre, August, Augie, and even Chief, looked up in amazement.

August laughed uneasily. "It's a little trick. We do it with magnets. Augie, would you mind waiting out in the car? It's time to take you home for lunch."

Augie dashed through the door with relief. As it slammed shut behind him, the nails and screws fell back down to the floor.

That night, August and Odile argued about Augie. They had spent the most challenging four years of their lives coping with Augie's unexplained abilities. Miraculously, they had kept it mostly a secret by executing a precise choreography of getting the child in and out of public places during those moments when nothing was likely to happened. Odile had been home-schooling Augie rather than send him to pre-school with other children.

But they were running out of energy and patience, and felt they needed help. It came down to Odile wanting to take Augie to a doctor and August wanting to take him to the priest at St. Joseph's, the local church.

August said, "What do doctors know about miracles? Nothing? We should take him to Father LeGrande."

But Odile said, "What if he has a rare disease? There could be some medicine for it."

"Odile, there's no cure for defying gravity."

It so happened that Father LeGrande, the pastor, was away on retreat that week, so August spoke with the assistant pastor, a young priest by the name of Father D'Antonio, who everybody called Father Dan for short. Father Dan agreed to come to the Boudreaux household and meet with Augie.

Odile ran around frantically that day cleaning and baking. By afternoon the house smelled like Pledge and chocolate chip cookies. August closed the store early and came home.

"Well now, Augie, how are you today?" said Father Dan, settling down on the sofa with a cup of coffee-and-chicory mixed with scalded milk, and a plate of cookies in front of him.

"I can make things go in the air," Augie said.

"I heard. What great fun," said Father Dan, who spoke like he didn't really believe it at all. Augie liked Father Dan's friendly smile and tanned face. He was so different from Father LeGrande, who had a large red face and was always blowing his nose.

August said, "But not just anything. Metal things."

"Metal objects? Could you give me a little demonstration?" said Father Dan kindly.

They were expecting this. On the shiny coffee table August set out a three-inch nail. Augie looked hard at the nail, his tongue protruding from the side of his mouth as he concentrated. After several seconds the nail started to vibrate, and then it rose into the air until it hit the ceiling, and stayed there.

Father Dan looked from the nail to Augie and back to the nail several times. "Amazing," he said slowly.

Augie smiled and the nail started to fall. "The table!" gasped Odile. August caught the nail in his large hand.

Father Dan's coffee cup rattled slightly as he took a sip. Augie and Annette went back to staring at the plate of cookies.

"Do the objects always fall back down?" Father Dan asked.

"They fall down after he stops thinking about them," said Odile.

"I see."

"Except..."

"Yes?"

August cleared his throat, as though self-conscious. "He did it outside once, with a screwdriver, and it kept going up and up until we couldn't see it anymore. And it never came back."

Father Dan looked at him thoughtfully. "It never came back," he repeated. "Augie, do you know where the screwdriver went?"

Augie shrugged. "I don't know where it went."

"I wonder if I could see you do this, outside?" said Father Dan.

They went into the back yard where August set the nail in the grass. Augie concentrated on the nail until it rose and rose and became a tiny speck in the sky and then it was out of sight.

"I can't believe what I'm witnessing," said Father Dan quietly. "If someone told me I wouldn't believe it."

They went back into the house with Father Dan shaking his head in bewilderment.

He spoke softly but excitedly. "I'm going to give you my opinion of this, but I must warn you, my opinion will be different from Father LeGrande's."

"Fair enough," said August.

"I believe your son was sent here by God to help with our terrible crime problem," said Father Dan.

"Crime?" August and Odile said it together.

"Imagine, if you will, a man about to commit a robbery with a gun, and then imagine the gun is yanked from his hand and flies into the air, never to be seen again. Imagine two men about to engage in a fight with knives, and then picture the knives flying out of their hands and into the air. Do you see what I mean? Imagine a man threatening a woman with a gun or a knife and the same thing happens. All over the city, imagine guns and knives and brass knuckles and pipes and all the things that kids use for weapons are flying into the air. Think of what that would do to the crime and violence that we have here in our city."

Odile looked scared to death. "Wouldn't that be dangerous for little Augie?" she said.

"Of course, I'm not recommending that he do this now. You need to raise him and take good care of him until he is old enough. Then, one day, the Lord will let you know when it's time."

August and Odile looked at each other with bewildered expressions. August said, "Just for the record, what would Father LeGrande say?"

Father Dan became very serious. "I think that Father LeGrande would say that Satan has taken over little Augie. But, you see, Father LeGrande, bless his heart, sees the devil in everything. Whereas me, I see the Lord in everything. Which do you prefer?"

August narrowed his eyes. "I'll have to think about it."

Father Dan stood up. "I have one more very important suggestion. Speak to Father LeGrande if you wish, but do not tell anyone else. Especially the newspapers."

"Yes, Father," said Odile.

After the priest left, August sat on the kitchen floor by the wall, trying to make sense of what he had just heard.

++++++

A tall teenage boy lounged on a lawn of green grass in the shade of a pecan tree. Arranged in front of him were several items that were at least partly made of metal: a hammer, a saw, an oil can and an old bicycle seat. The boy focused his attention on the objects one at a time, and each one rose slightly into the air and hovered a few feet off the ground. The boy took a bite from a snow cone, watching the objects vibrate slightly as they hovered. Then, one by one, they descended slowly to the ground.

"Gotcha," said a female voice behind him.

Augie Boudreaux whirled around. A young woman about his age, dressed in shorts and a tank top, held a video camera. "Rosemary, what are you doing?" he said.

"I finally caught you doing one of your tricks, Augie." Rosemary Landaiche held the camera close to her like it was a precious object.

"My parents are going to be very mad if they find out," said Augie.

She came and sat near him on the grass. "How come those things don't disappear into the sky like they used to?"

"I can make them go up a short distance and hold them," said Augie. "But if I want to, I can let them go up until they don't come back."

"Show me. Pretty please? I'll put the camera down."

Augie tossed the old bicycle seat away from the shade of the tree. It was red and white, with a large S stamped on the top. Augie stared at the seat, which had a metal post, and it rose into the air. It rose and rose without stopping until Augie and Rosemary got tired of tilting their necks to look up in the sky.

"What if the stuff all comes back one day?"

"It won't."

Rosemary smiled at Augie and stretched her long legs out on the grass. "Where'd ya get the snowball?"

"Over by the hardware store. What are you going to do with that film?"

"Oh, I might be willing to trade it for something," she said.

Augie sighed, "Okay, I'll buy you a snowball."

"Ha. This film is worth a lot more than that," said Rosemary.

"This isn't a joke, Rosemary. You are one of the few people outside of the family who know what I do, mainly because you're my sister's friend and you're around all the time."

"Augie, you know I wouldn't show it to anybody," said Rosemary.

"In that case, why don't you let me hold onto it for you?"

"Not so fast. I have a little problem. My Mom bought me a nice new prom dress but I don't have a date. How would you like to take me to the Dominican senior prom?"

Dominican was a popular girl's high school in New Orleans. Augie thought about the offer and realized that he actually wouldn't mind taking Rosemary. She had a reputation for being bossy, but she was also very attractive.

"All right. It's a deal. When do I get the film?"

"After the prom." Rosemary winked at him. "Wait until you see my dress."

On the night of the prom, Augie and Rosemary walked out of the lobby of Hotel Monteleone in the French Quarter after an evening of dancing. Augie wore a tuxedo with a maroon crushed-velvet jacket. She wore a black, clingy dress that was cut low in the front.

They walked, hand in hand, down Royal to Bienville and then over to Decatur. The side streets were dark and nearly deserted. Most of the tourists were either still in bars or back at their hotels.

When they were a half-block from Decatur Street, a man stepped from between two parked cars.

"What's the hurry, folks?" the man said.

Augie tightened his grip on Rosemary's hand and tried to go around the man. The man moved and blocked them. He was tall and wore an undershirt and several gold chains around his neck. A second man moved in behind them. They were trapped.

"Nice prom dress," said the second man. "How much a dress like that set you back?"

"What do you want?" said Augie.

The second man leaned close to Rosemary. "I want that dress."

What happened next went so fast Augie could hardly believe it was real. The man circled his left arm around Rosemary and drew her away from the wall. At the same time he pulled out a long knife and held it to her throat.

"Ever seen a k-bar, dude?"

Augie had seen the knife in a Soldier of Fortune magazine ad. It was a Marine Corps K-Bar. Rosemary's face turned white with fear.

The first man spoke. "This is real simple, prom boy. You hand over your prom night cash and we let the little lady go."

"After I get the dress," the second man said. With the knife edge pressed against Rosemary's throat, the man slid his other hand into her dress. Her eyes widened and she started to make a sound.

The first man held up a gun. "You're out of time, prom boy. Let's go."

"Augie, the weapons," Rosemary said.

"Yeah, we got weapons, and they hurt," said the second man.

Rosemary clenched her teeth. "Augie, goddamit, the weapons."

Of course, the gun and the knife. Augie knew what he had to do. He focused his attention on the two weapons. It had to work. And it did. As if yanked by an invisible string the knife and the gun were torn from the

23

hands of the two men and rose into the night sky. Augie kept his thoughts on the weapons as the men stared up at them in amazement.

Rosemary, taking advantage of the distraction, raised one foot as high as she could and slammed her sharp heel into the second man's foot. The man screamed and jumped back.

Augie grabbed Rosemary's hand and they ran. The men didn't chase them. Rosemary reached down and pulled off her heels.

When they reached Decatur Street, they ran breathlessly into a bar filled with people. A burly bouncer said, "Got some I.D?"

On the way home, Augie and Rosemary still trembled from the experience. "You know," said Augie, "I've been reading in the papers about all the crime that's going on around New Orleans, but I've never seen it close up."

"My heart is still pounding," said Rosemary.

"I read that in places like the Ninth Ward and the Desire Projects, people live with violence all the time," said Augie. "Can you imagine?"

"Fortunately, I don't know anyone who lives there."

"We know one person: Father Dan. Remember him? He got transferred to St. Rita's in the Ninth Ward."

"I'd forgotten about him. I wonder how he's doing."

Augie steered the car down River Road, leaving the city limits and heading toward their neighborhood by the levee.

"Did I ever tell you what he said about me?"

"What?"

"That I should be a crime fighter. He said, way back when I was like, four years old, that I should go around and stop crime by making the guns and knives go up in the air."

"Just like tonight."

"Exactly."

"Augie, you probably saved our lives."

He looked at her. "Maybe I should give Father Dan a call."

A few days later Augie called Father Dan and made arrangements to visit him at his rectory in the Ninth Ward. He borrowed his father's old pickup and drove across town to an extremely poor and violent section just east of downtown.

They went for a walk along a graffiti-smeared, depressed boulevard. Augie told him everything that had happened the night of the prom. He ended with, "I think I'd like to help out. This city's going to be ruined if we don't stop the crime."

Father Dan looked at the eager teenager and said, "I need to warn you, this could be dangerous."

"I want to try it. The other night it felt so good to stop those guys. You should've seen the looks on their faces. They were used to dealing with cops and guns, but they didn't see this coming."

Augie could see that Father Dan still had the friendly smile that he remembered, but now he looked older, and tired, like he had seen a lot of unpleasant things.

"Okay," said Father Dan. "Friday night. Can you meet me right here?"

When Friday evening came, Augie was at the rectory with his father's truck. "Where do we start?"

"Desire Projects," said Father Dan. "The worst battleground in the city and possibly in the country right now. Did you know that New Orleans has the distinction of having one of the most corrupt and inefficient police departments in the country?"

They got into the pickup truck and drove off. As Augie made the turn onto Desire Parkway and drove through the infamous housing project he was sickened at the sight of the dark dilapidated buildings, the trash, the broken cars, and worst of all, the children walking sullenly in groups, looking mean and hard.

They came to a halt in the darkness beneath an oak tree, next to a small park filled with weeds and broken glass. Augie turned off the engine.

"What now?"

"We wait," said Father Dan.

They listened to a baby crying somewhere and the sounds of people arguing. Ten minutes later Augie felt the truck vibrate and realized it was the booming bass speakers of a car that passed slowly by them. It was a shiny car with windows rolled up.

"Drug dealer," said Father Dan. "They're the only ones with money around here."

The car pulled over to the curb about thirty feet ahead of them. A door opened and a young man was pushed out of the car.

"Get ready," said Father Dan.

Augie saw a hand emerge from the car, it held a gun, pointed at the man who was sitting on the grass, looking dazed.

"Now!"

Augie focused his attention on the gun like a laser. It was yanked into the air from the hand that held it. The man on the ground watched it rise up and out of sight. He got up and ran. The car door closed and the vehicle tore away from the curb. Augie kept his thoughts on the gun until he was sure it was gone for good.

"You just saved a life," Father Dan said.

"Wish I coulda seen the look on that guy's face," said Augie.

A half-hour later they were parked down the street from a loud night club, watching four men huddled near the curb. Suddenly one man pushed another roughly and the four men backed away from each other. As if on cue, the four men reached into their baggy shirts and pulled out large hand weapons.

"Machine pistols. Hurry." Father's Dan's voice was urgent.

Augie bored into them. He had a clear view of the weapons. They rose into the air. All four of the men watched the useless weapons sail into the night sky. Then they looked at each other, their eyes filled with fear and distrust. They fled.

"You saved four more lives, at least for now."

Augie smiled. "This is better than a video game."

For the next three weeks, Augie and Father Dan went on a crime-fighting spree throughout the Desire Projects and the Ninth Ward. Criminals never knew exactly when or where it would happen.

A robbery attempt was thwarted when the gunmen lost their weapons as they were about to enter a convenience store. A young girl on a playground was about to be raped at knifepoint by two teenagers when she, and the rapists, watched the knife disappear into the fog. In a bizarre incident on Desire Parkway, two rival gangs faced off from behind parked cars in a made-for-TV shootout when suddenly their guns flew into the air. Machine pistols, 9mm handguns, and even an Uzi were unceremoniously yanked from surprised hands and pulled into the sky. The gangs dispersed with fear on their faces. One woman watching from her window made the sign of the cross and lit a candle in front of her Blessed Virgin Mary statue. Throughout these episodes, no one spotted Augie and Father Dan sitting in a darkened car or standing in the shadows of an alley or walking through a park.

The city was buzzing with rumors and speculation. The chief of police held a news conference and ruled out UFOs as an explanation and emphasized over and over the sudden drop in crime. The police department, he insisted, was getting better at fighting crime. Of course, no one believed it.

The newspapers and television stations scrambled to get pictures of the phenomena but they were always too late. It seemed everyone had an opinion about why the bizarre incidents were happening. An elderly woman appeared on the evening news saying that God was "stepping in to kick some butt." Someone else said that a planet of superior beings was sucking all of the weapons off the Earth, and conflict as we know it today was coming to an end.

Then tragedy struck the Boudreaux family. Augie was home with his mother when they got a call from the police: there had been a shooting at the hardware store. Augie, Odile and Annette rushed there as fast as they could and found yellow police tape already surrounding the place. The family insisted on seeing for themselves. Since the parish sheriff knew the Boudreauxs he let them in. August Boudreaux was slumped on the floor with two shots through the chest. Odile fainted. Augie helped her, his hands shaking as he did so. It took every ounce of control to keep the entire inventory of the hardware store from bursting through the roof.

Over the next couple of days, the sheriff gave them bits and pieces of information: the killers stole cash from the cash register plus six DeWalt cordless power drills; a witness who was making doughnuts next door at McKenzie's saw two black teenagers leave the store with the power drills and get into a black Cadillac with a rusted right rear quarter-panel and no hubcaps. The license plate was covered with mud. The witness said he saw them laughing as they tore out of the alley and careened around the corner, heading toward the levee.

The witness also saw something else: one of the teenagers had a scar on his cheek in the shape of the letter J.

Days later, after the wake and the funeral, Augie went to the hardware store and looked at the blood stains on the counter, on the cash register, and on the wall. He felt a new feeling inside of him, a kind of rage. It was a physical sensation that filled him with something hot and uncontrollable. It seemed to lift him off the ground. As he stood by the counter, where the two killers must have stood, he felt the rage escape his body and swirl around him like a tornado. Practically everything in the store went into the air: hammers, saws, screwdrivers, nails, screws, staples, staple guns, wrenches, power saws, lug nuts, tackle boxes. It all rose and slammed against the ceiling and ricocheted off the walls and flew through the air in a giant vortex. Nothing touched him, everything flew around him, and when an object came close it was repelled by some protective force that surrounded his body.

Then, as quickly as it had started, it died down. One by one the items glided to the floor. Augie felt stronger than he had ever felt in his life, and incredibly light at the same time. He was ready to return to the streets.

When he met with Father Dan late one evening, the priest said to him, "Are you sure you can do this?"

"Yes."

"Augie, I just want to remind you of something. This is about saving lives, it's not about revenge."

"I know."

They continued their crime-fighting spree. Augie was quiet, almost sullen, throughout all of it, until one day. They were driving through a rough section of the Ninth Ward during the middle of the afternoon because Father Dan wanted to show Augie a certain neighborhood and to find a stake-out spot. Suddenly Augie saw something that grabbed his attention: a black Cadillac with a rusted quarter panel, which fit the description of the getaway car that the killers of his father had used. Augie slowed and scanned the people on the sidewalk, and what he saw made him almost break the steering wheel from gripping it so tightly. A young man was handing a DeWalt cordless drill, still new in the box, to another man, and accepting what looked like cash in return. The young man had a distinctive scar on his cheek, in the shape of the letter J. Augie felt a rush of anger, but he kept it to himself while a plan formed in his mind.

A few nights later, on a night they were planning to go out, Augie called Father Dan on the phone.

"We have a problem," Augie said.

"What is it?"

"Someone from my neighborhood knows what's going on, and he wants to get me on film so he can sell it to the media."

"Who?"

"His name is Claude Landaiche, the brother of my sister's friend."

Father Dan winced. "How did he find out?"

"A couple of months ago, my sister's friend, Rosemary, took a video of me doing stuff in the back yard. We made a deal and she promised not to show it to anyone. But her brother found the tape."

Father Dan was silent for a moment.

"We'd better lay low for a while; let things cool down," he said.

"Are you sure?"

"I can't risk getting you into trouble. There's no telling what people would do if they connected you to this."

Augie said, "Okay, you're the boss." It was exactly what he was hoping Father Dan would say. Augie wanted this night to himself. He wanted to go without Father Dan because he had a particular stake-out in mind. It was true that Claude Landaiche found the video that Rosemary had taken, and he wanted to take more footage so he could sell it to media. He offered to split the proceeds with Augie. Augie had said no deal; everything had to be kept a secret. Augie figured Claude would drop the matter.

At eleven o'clock in the evening, after the house had been dark and quiet for a while, Augie got a pair of binoculars out of his closet and slid through his bedroom window. He quietly pushed his bicycle out of the side yard to the front walk and then started pedaling toward the river. A half-block behind him, Claude Landaiche started his car and followed.

Augie crossed River Road and pushed his bike up the grassy slope to the top of the levee. He pedaled rapidly through the warm night air, so humid he could feel the moisture building up on his skin. When he got to the corner of Carrollton and St. Charles, he coasted down the levee and steered onto the avenue just as a street car was rounding the corner. Claude followed from a block behind. Augie rode past Audubon Park, turned right onto Henry Clay and then stopped at a long, narrow shotgun house that his friend, Roby Mouton, rented with his girlfriend. They had gone to Destin, Florida, for a little vacation, and Roby had been letting Augie use his old Ford work van while they were away.

Augie parked his bike on the side of the house. It was the old style, built off the ground. He reached up under it and retrieved the key to the van. He also removed a small canvas bag. He got into the van and drove off. He went across town, over the Industrial Canal and into the dark, combat-zone streets of the Ninth Ward. Claude followed him all the way. Augie went to the intersection where he had seen the black Cadillac with the rusted quarter-panel. It wasn't there. He circled the block and then returned to a spot across the street and down from where he had seen the car. Claude Landaiche parked on the opposite side of the street, but further back, with a clear view of Augie's van.

Augie saw the Cadillac after about twenty minutes. One headlight was burned out. It coasted into the vacant spot across the street. The driver and another young man got out, illuminated briefly by a street lamp. Augie leaned back in the darkness of the van and raised the binoculars to his eyes. He focused first on the driver's face, then on the second person. The second person had the scar, the letter J, plain as could be.

Augie reached around the seat and unzipped the canvas bag he had retrieved from Roby's house. It contained a .45 caliber, military-style sidearm that Roby's brother had purchased at a pawn shop in Mississippi. Augie shoved a full clip into the handle of the weapon and stuffed it into his pocket, and pulled his dark, loose-fitting tee-shirt over it.

Claude Landaiche also had equipment: an expensive-looking video camera that he hoisted up to his shoulders as he got out of his car.

The two men who were the object of Augie's interest proceeded down the sidewalk. At the corner, where a street light had been busted, the men stopped in the semi-darkness. They conversed for a moment, then turned back the way they had come.

Augie saw the men duck suddenly into a dark storefront. He knew something was up. He saw a glint of steel. They had weapons. Something was about to happen.

Augie crossed the street. The two men were watching the sidewalk. Then they moved from their hiding place, guns raised.

Augie removed his weapon from his pocket and held it in his hands. He felt absolutely fearless. They didn't stand a chance, he thought. They were as good as dead. He pictured himself pointing his weapon at the man with the J on his cheek. He imagined squeezing the trigger and watching the bullet tear through the man's chest. His intention was to aim exactly at the spot in the chest where they had shot his father. Then a knot formed in his stomach when he saw the target of their advances: it was Claude Landaiche, standing between two parked cars, holding a movie camera.

Augie saw the men approach Claude; there was no doubt they wanted the camera. He cursed himself for not taking Claude seriously. He must have rented the damn camera, Augie thought. Augie's plan had been to shoot immediately and then leave the scene. But now Claude complicated things. He would of course catch Augie committing a murder. But the alternative was to stop the men by using his powers, and Claude would get that on film. One was almost as bad as the other.

In an instant he made up his mind. "Claude, look out!" he shouted. Then he focused on the weapons, while still holding his own pistol in his right hand. But something went wrong. He locked his attention on the guns of the two men, which he could see clearly, but nothing happened. The guns didn't fly from their hands. He tried harder. Nothing. His powers were failing him! He began to panic.

The man with the J fired. Claude went down. Augie screamed. Then the men turned their faces to the new threat, now tense and alert, and saw Augie with his weapon. They started to turn their guns toward him. Augie saw it unfolding as if in slow motion. He felt nothing but hot anger and again focused all of his energy on the guns now almost pointing at him. But he could not make them sail away into the night sky as he had been doing for weeks. His powers had stopped. He saw the muzzles of the weapons, one of them still smoking.

Augie raised his weapon and fired twice. Both men went down. A bullet in each chest.

Augie ran to Claude. He was dead. Augie knelt by Claude and shook him, then he started crying.

After a moment Augie heard a very faint sound: a clatter of metal and hard plastic. He looked. In the street, a screwdriver had fallen to the pavement. Augie was puzzled. It was followed by nail, which hit the concrete with a light ping. Then a Schwinn bicycle seat landed with a thud. Then a familiar-looking knife fell into the circle of light. Augie recognized it as a Marine Corps K-Bar.

He heard voices, neighbors coming out to see who had been shot. Something else fell, and a pistol lay in the street. Another one landed next to it, and bounced and went off. People screamed and started running. Two more knives fell, then several other weapons, including an Uzi.

Augie had a sick feeling that he knew what was happening. He ran along the sidewalk, dazed, still holding his own weapon.

Someone yelled, "Call the police. There's the killer."

Augie threw the pistol down. "No! He killed my father. I've been helping you people."

Then it rained weapons. They fell from the sky in a shower of steel, like someone had turned over a chest of arms and emptied the contents. Pistols, knives, pipes, machine guns. They clattered on cars, rooftops, streets and sidewalks, and collected in piles of metal. Some of them went off as they landed. Augie ran for the van. He saw several boys fighting over the fallen weapons. Something hit Augie hard on the head, and blood ran down his face. He got into the van. The sound was deafening.

He threw himself down on the floor, and held his ears and cried. Tears and blood streamed down his face. Above the roar he heard police sirens.

SEEKING REFUGE AT THE PALM COURT
An Evening in New Orleans, June 24, 2006

I parked a block off Decatur Street, feeling proud of myself for finding free street parking on a Saturday night in the French Quarter. I was in town for the American Library Association annual meeting and, being a native of the area, decided to see for myself how things were going in the city. It was my third visit to New Orleans since the hurricane: I was here last October, again in April, and now June. I felt a need to do my own personal assessment of the city's recovery.

It was still early, and hot, even though heavy gray clouds had gathered over the city. Rain was coming. A strong wind blew off the river and whipped up dust from the streets. Tourists with cigarettes and tattoos swarmed the sidewalks and crowded the entrances of bad restaurants with lots of neon and numerous television sets and good air conditioning. I was reminded of a question my son had once asked me when he was about six years old. It was right after nine-eleven and he was discovering the word terrorist, but he was confusing it with tourist, and he said "What's the difference, Dad?" I sighed and said "I don't know."

I walked up Decatur to St. Louis Street and turned left. My destination was the Napoleon House, a personal favorite of mine and one of the world's great watering holes by any standard of measure. For most of the afternoon at the library convention I had been dreaming of their signature spicy tomato-and-vodka drink with a string bean in it, perhaps accompanied by a muffaletta, an Italian sandwich prized by the locals. But it was not to be: the Napoleon House was closed for the evening. Not a good sign. It never closed early. I had already noticed, during this visit to New Orleans, that the St. Charles streetcar was still not running; and now this. The city is definitely on life support.

I continued down Chartres to Jackson Square. A wedding party was trying to have pictures taken in front of the cathedral while buskers set up battered equipment for a night of performing. Very dirty people lounging on benches bummed cigarettes off each other. Sparkling well-scrubbed people stood in little clutches deciding where to eat and saying things like "So which one is the Pontalba House?"

I passed through the square and returned to Decatur Street, since it contained many of my own reference points for judging how the city had changed since my youth. The Central Grocery was closed, as expected, since it was a daytime food store, noteworthy for being the place where the muffaletta was invented. My mouth watered. I was not going to be denied my dinner of choice. Tujague's was open and seemed to have a good crowd. I was pleased, but didn't want to spend a lot of money dining alone; there was something depressing about that.

When I reached Decatur and St. Philip I found the Market Cafe. This establishment sits on the odd wedge-shaped property where Decatur splits into N. Peters. I believe it was the site of the Morning Call, a coffee stand that competed for years with the now-more-famous Cafe du Monde.

I entered the patio of the Market Cafe, thinking I would at least investigate the menu. A four-piece jazz band entertained diners beneath a broad awning that stretched from one side of the wedge to the other. There was inside seating, but it seemed cool enough to sit outside, and there were empty tables, which meant no waiting. I selected a table with a good view of both the band and the river, which was visible through an open space between buildings on the other side of the street. That same stiff breeze that I had felt earlier blew through the patio and sent napkins and bits of trash rolling past the guitar player's constantly-tapping foot. I again smelled rain.

I had only one question for the waitress after browsing the menu. "How are your muffalettas?"

"Excellent," she said. Of course.

"Okay I'll take the muffaletta."

"Half or whole?"

"Half."

"And to drink?"

"How are your Bloody Marys?" I cringed when I said it; I had never liked that name. An old friend named Mary used to call them Jolly Marys, but I didn't think the waitress would know what I was talking about.

"It's our best selling drink," she said. Of course. She knew just what to say to me.

"I'll take one."

"House or market?" she asked.

When I didn't answer right away she said, "Market is the good stuff."

I took it as a challenge: am I the sort who takes mere house liquor in his drink? "Market," I stated. I could not interpret the amused expression that crossed her face as she wrote the order in her little pad.

The other patrons seemed to be visitors, like myself. There were two women, each dining alone, each with tote bags from the library convention. I wondered why they didn't introduce themselves and enjoy some shop talk about libraries. Maybe they had been doing that all day and were sick of it. A family of six wore gaudy Bourbon Street t-shirts. A white-haired couple chain-smoked cigarettes at the edge of the patio, downwind from my table.

The band seemed kind of bored. They mostly played the well-worn New Orleans standards that all the bands played. A beat-up wooden sign announced that they worked for tips only. The drummer stared over the crowd toward the river as he played, lost in thought but never losing his place in the tune. The bass player checked his cell phone for messages after each song, perhaps hoping to be summoned for a paying gig. The guitar player wore dark glasses and a dark hat and sat hunched over his instrument with a lit cigarette sticking out of the side of his mouth. The sax player sat next to him, the only black member of the group, providing the big sound that echoed throughout the patio and drew people off the sidewalk.

The manager of the restaurant came out to the patio from time to time to visit patrons. He wore a big smile and a small mustache, and his graying hair had been dyed some kind of brownish-reddish color. When he passed the band he would hum whatever tune they were playing and snap his fingers in rhythm. Every once in a while he carried menus out to the sidewalk and called out his specials to passers-by. I heard him shout across the street to the dishwasher who had stepped outside in his damp apron to smoke a cigarette.

Beyond the patio of the Market Cafe, in the very tip of the wedge between Decatur and N. Peters, stood a cluster of crepe myrtle trees in bloom. Suddenly a gust of wind caught the trees just right and, Pop!, pink blossoms burst like confetti and swirled through the patio and landed in drinks and came to rest on crawfish bisque and some fell to the floor and mingled with cigarette butts and discarded napkins. By this time my drink had been served to me--strong and very spicy--and I sat back to enjoy the show. Even the musicians reacted to Nature's accompaniment by tightening up their loose, laid back, heat-induced, rhythmic style. I saw the drummer now looking beyond the edges of the patio with something like excitement, or merely interest, in his eyes.

My muffaletta came and it was perfect: layers of imported ham and salami, topped with a salad of crushed olives and roasted peppers, and encased in warm bread. I was content and happy that I had found something a local might enjoy: a bite of tasty food and a strong drink and some jazz tunes, all at a modest price and without waiting. This was how the locals liked their city: cheap and good and fast.

The band played a short, Dixieland version of C Jam Blues and then took a break. I was pleasantly surprised to note that no juke box music came on to fill the dreaded dead air that existed while a band was on break. It was pleasantly quiet on the patio. The drummer ate an ice cream sandwich while the bass player talked on his cell phone. The guitarist stepped into the bar across the street and I didn't see where the sax player went. I ate my meal and felt my mind and body slow down. No one was in a hurry here. It was too hot to be in a hurry.

Soon the librarians left and the family left and the chain-smoking couple left, all to be replaced by other diners. New faces. More of them. Most tables were filled now. I was the lone holdover from the previous wave. I became the old timer on the patio, the tenured diner who knew a good muffaletta when he saw one. It was a darker, too. I could see the famous Tujague's sign lighting up against a heavy gray cloud. I was aware that time had passed without checking the time. The band returned for the next set and launched into more standards.

I didn't actually see the first few drops of rain; instead I saw pedestrians holding out their palms and looking skyward. Then I saw a few others duck beneath the awnings that covered most of the sidewalks. Then the drops were plainly visible, just a few at first, then more, then the skies opened up. Fat raindrops crashed to the pavement and awnings and parked cars. Each drop caused a sharp splat and millions of drops created a roar. The gutters filled with rushing water. The air became a swirling bath of rainwater and steam. A powerful and familiar smell hit me. It was the rain and the river, and the streets of the neighborhood where I grew up and the pecan trees and St Augustine grass in my front yard. Every rainstorm, I remembered, carried all of those smells in a little memory capsule. It was then I noticed, with almost a laugh, the grains of uncooked rice in the salt shakers. How could that old trick possibly work in such humid weather?

The band, positioned on the downwind side of the patio, didn't miss a beat as the rain fell. On my side of the patio, the wind-driven rain slanted onto the tables near the edge. I picked up my meal and darted to an empty table near the band. Two waiters pulled tables in while patrons picked up their food and drinks and purses and shopping bags and moved across the patio.

My new seat provided me with a side view of the band, and, beyond, a view down Decatur Street to the old Jax Brewery. My drink by this time was nothing but a cup of mostly melted ice cubes. The waitress sensed my dilemma and appeared at my side as if by magic. I shrugged. "I guess I'm having another," I said.

"Well, it is raining," she said.

What a treat, I thought, to wait out a New Orleans rainstorm in a patio bar with good booze and a live band. This was living!

The rain continued for fifteen or twenty minutes and then slowed to a drizzle and then stopped altogether. I could hear water gurgling in the gutters, and could see a sheen of flowing water on the streets reflecting the Tujague's sign and the traffic lights.

People once again filled the sidewalks. The manager went out with his menus as the band started playing When The Saints Go Marching In. As the sound of the big sax filtered out of the patio, a group of college kids started dancing on the sidewalk. I suspected they might be cheerleaders when I saw their routine become very acrobatic. Two women leapt into the air in rhythm with the music and were caught and twirled by tall men with muscled bodies and short hair. Then the sax player handed the solo to the guitarist, who created a danceable yet soulful jig out of that tired tune. Even the bass player reached deep and possibly for the first time that evening pleased himself by finding a riff that satisfied. I gave the band a good tip.

A thought occurred to me about New Orleans at that moment. It was my own little riff. It was the idea that the best way to visit the city was to let it visit you. To sit in one spot and let weather and humanity and music and trash flow around you like a lazy river. I think that was what I had always done here without realizing it. I had to go away in order to see it.

My second drink was now empty and I decided it was time to move on. Out of curiosity, I asked the waitress where she was from. Pittsburg was the answer. I wondered if there were any locals still left in the French Quarter.

I continued up Decatur Street, noticing a striking increase in light and noise coming from some of the bars compared to what I could recall from my last visit to the Quarter, perhaps four or five years ago. Some establishments had become caverns of light: floors, ceilings and walls bathed in noxious hues of fluorescent color. Television screens, mirrors, and shiny bar stools completed the visual spectacle while my ears were assaulted by booming bass notes coming from enormous loudspeakers. I was certain the sounds could be heard by tugboat operators clear out in the middle of the Mississippi River.

But I walked for a few more blocks instead of turning back because there was a place I had in mind, a reliable oasis of civilized good cheer, a local hangout, a barometer to measure either the decline or rebirth of New Orleans, depending on your point of view. It was the Palm Court.

The Palm Court is an anomaly in the French Quarter. It's only open a few days each week, and only until about eleven o'clock. And every year it closes for the summer. The owner and founder, an Englishwoman named Nina Buck, is a great lover of New Orleans music and wanted to create an establishment for showcasing the best in local jazz talent, especially the older musicians who play a rapidly disappearing style. In that respect the Palm Court is somewhat like Preservation Hall, except that it has a full menu and a bar, and doesn't get the crush of tourists.

The Palm Court is charming and understated: a simple tiled floor, exposed brick walls, ceiling fans, a few plants, soft lighting. Paintings and photographs of jazz musicians hang from the walls, along with a collection of record album covers, many of them produced and released by Nina's husband. The building itself had been a food warehouse for decades before the Bucks bought and renovated the place and opened the Palm Court in 1989. By New Orleans standards, that's young. But it quickly became an institution.

Within moments after walking in and finding an empty stool at the mahogany bar, I knew I had happened into the Palm Court on a special night: it was the last night of the season before Miss Nina, as she is called by everyone, closes the bar for the summer. I learned this from a gentleman sitting on my right who, with his wife, had come into town from the West Bank (of the Mississippi River, that is). I didn't catch their names, but I'll call him Ed, for now. Ed was a true local, and a regular at the Palm Court. He told me right off that he and his wife were "Katrina survivors." Ed knew the names of all the band members, and he even knew many of the patrons sitting around the bar.

Miss Nina was all over the place. She wore a blue-and-white print dress and flitted among the tables, greeting people and occasionally doing a dance step or two in front of the band. She served drinks from behind the bar, answered the phone, delivered things from the kitchen to the dining room, all with a natural elegance and charm. She was an Englishwoman who had become a classic New Orleans hostess.

Between songs, Nina mounted the stage to introduce the musicians: four old men and one young clarinet player. She gave an especially warm introduction for Lionel Ferbos, one of the living legends of the New Orleans music scene. Lionel was born in 1911 and today, at age 95, is still a working musician, playing trumpet in bands on a weekly basis. Nina explained that Lionel had lost his house and was displaced by Katrina but was back in town thanks to a lot of support from friends and fans and family. The crowd applauded warmly, and the band started their next tune. Lionel sat with his thin legs crossed one over the other, dressed in a white shirt and blue tie. The white fringes of hair on his temples contrasted with his black-rimmed spectacles. He blew big, warm tones in a calm, unhurried way. This was Dixieland playing in that relaxed, lazy style that, paradoxically, was both loose and precise.

Later in the evening, new people started pouring into the bar. Ed named several of them for me: they were all musicians just getting off work at Preservation Hall, and were stopping in for closing night at the Palm Court. It felt suddenly like a place of refuge. These people, who had only recently sought shelter from Katrina, now, I fancied, sought shelter from a different kind of threat: the disappearance of a distinct New Orleans subculture. I imagined these musicians to be the last holdouts against a tide of noise and bad taste, the last Dixieland players in the last bastion of Dixieland playing. Ed introduced me to a large man with a white hat and sunglasses who had been playing bass for sixty-eight years. This was his life.

Nina greeted all of them by name and made sure they had seats and drinks and food. The conversations surrounding me were all about local things: music, jobs, houses, recovery, FEMA, the mayor and his bad jokes. One woman who worked for a local medical school explained that the city had lost half its doctors. Another talked about how long she had to look before she found an affordable apartment. One man told me he had just interviewed for a job at the University of Washington and wanted to know about the jazz scene in Seattle. I told him about my favorite clubs and the diversity of jazz styles you can hear and the Earshot Jazz Festival. I asked him why he was moving, and he said "It's time."

Finally, the band played their last song of the evening and took a bow that was more like a farewell, and then packed up the instruments and emptied the tip jar. It was closing time, for the summer, at the Palm Court. Miss Nina hugged old friends and kissed them on their cheeks. I said goodbye to Ed and his wife and, with some reluctance, left the bar. For a moment, I wanted to be a local again. I wanted to be in that bar, with the regulars, hashing over old times and ruminating about the future. But, alas, it wasn't my station in life at the moment.

I retraced my steps back down Decatur. I couldn't resist stopping in the Cafe du Monde for a cafe au lait and an order of beignets. The patio crowd was of the tired, rumpled, sweaty, late-night variety. To them this was a foreign country: exotic, hot, humid, noisy, dirty, rainy, layered with grime and powdered sugar and cooking fat. The glasses of ice water sweated and slid around the table top. The cafe au lait was perfectly prepared, the beignets were very fresh and warm. With each bite, I tasted home. Home was still here, in spite of everything

HOW I'M HANDLING MY MIDLIFE CRISIS

Reprinted from the Seattle Post-Intelligencer

Friday, July 8, 2005

BY **BILL BRANLEY**
SPECIAL TO THE POST-INTELLIGENCER

I turn 50 this year, and I am proud to report that I am not falling for those midlife crisis fantasies that seem to afflict less disciplined males than myself. You know the type: They climb tall mountains, buy sports cars, date women half their age. That's not for me. And my wife wouldn't go for it, anyway. Instead, I am going to proudly observe my half-century mark by NOT running the Seattle Marathon.

I'm sure many of my peers will be out there, staving off old age by huffing and puffing down the road, getting passed up by fortysomethings in tight running shorts. Sorry, I won't be joining you. There are at least a dozen good reasons for not running the Seattle Marathon. I'm giving you a dozen because, frankly, aren't you getting tired of Top 10 lists? I once had an authority figure who said "excuses are a dime a dozen." So here is my dime's worth of excuses.

1. I can run only 26.1 miles and not a yard more. My body stops at that point as a matter of principle.

2. My favorite rerun of "The Dick Van Dyke Show" is on television that morning. Do you remember the one where Laura had her baby?

3. I'm old enough to remember "The Dick Van Dyke Show." Wasn't it hilarious? Whatever happened to quality television?

4. I can't find the time to get together with my old Army buddies to go

"carbo loading." Hey, it worked when I was 22!

5. Marathon training interferes with my diet. I can't get enough of those Top Pot doughnuts.

6. I'll be so far behind in the race that I'll get stuck in rush-hour traffic on Monday morning. But wait -- if I'm running to work Monday, I'll get there faster than if I'm driving.

7. I'm planning to have a headache.

8. I may have a hangover from trying to get a headache.

9. I will be intimidated by all the seventysomethings who pass me up. Those guys need to get a life.

10. My running shorts from the last time I ran don't fit me anymore. People change, right?

11. I heard there was a hill.

12. I heard there were two hills.

I realize a few readers may dispute the appropriateness of some of my reasons. I hereby state that it is not the policy of this author to glamorize drinking and bad dieting and ill-fitting running shorts. But on certain people, they look pretty cool.

See you at the finish line!

GETTING AWAY

The McBee Motel Cottages sit at the corner of Van Buren and South Hemlock Streets in Cannon Beach, Oregon.

Of the words in the name, 'motel' is more accurate than 'cottages.' Two buildings arranged in an L-shape contain about a dozen connected units. A crunchy gravel drive loops past the units so you can pull your car to within six inches of your door if you are strongly opposed to walking. In the center of the complex is a grassy lawn with faux-Adirondack chairs around a fire pit. The scene looks cozy but unused. Our unit, at the end, has plenty of windows and light. There is a single bedroom with a queen bed, a living room with two sleeper sofas, a kitchen equipped with a corkscrew, and a bathroom. The spacious fireplace has a synthetic log, ready for lighting. I estimate the McBee cottages were built in the 1940s and have been meticulously maintained by some hard-working, underpaid handy person, probably a relative of the owner. When the handy person dies the whole enterprise will go to hell.

The four-hour trip from Seattle wasn't bad except for having to pass through Longview, Washington, in order to cross the Columbia River into Oregon. Longview is a classic American concrete city with little else but streets and parking lots and drab chain stores and lots of cars, most of them blaring noise from their open windows. I only mention it because if you are driving to Cannon Beach from Seattle you should find a route that goes anywhere but Longview.

Cannon Beach is a tidy village that has benefited from carefully written growth and development restrictions. It has a residential feel throughout, and the commercial buildings are relatively small and understated. Even my 12-year-old son observed that "there aren't any hotel chains here." I didn't see a single brand name I recognized on all of the inns, motels, guest houses and cottages that we passed. Nor on the restaurants and retail stores. Perhaps everything in town is owned by a single giant company headquartered in New York. However, I am being sloppy in my reporting: there was at least one store sign I recognized, for Birkenstock shoes. Apparently, some brand names are allowed in.

The beach is a short walk down Van Buren Street from our cottage. Thankfully, there are no roads to cross, just a peaceful stroll down a block of small houses. One house is called Wee Mist. Another has two ancient, rusted cannons in front. I wonder if they are the original cannons of Cannon Beach.

Upon reaching the shore I am surprised to see such a wide expanse of sand. I was expecting a small rocky shoreline. Beyond the sand is the roiling, rolling surf. The Pacific Ocean, at last! Looking south, I gaze at the largest freestanding rock formation I have ever seen. It's called haystack rock, and, yes, it looks exactly like a very large haystack. Further south I see more rock formations, and sand and forest, fading into a murky afternoon mist.

We go to dinner. My son and I have ribs; I have a Guinness. My daughter has a small pizza and my wife has rotisserie chicken and rice. Surprisingly, the vegetables that come with our meals are not overcooked. We take leftovers back to our rooms. On the way we stop at a small market and buy marshmallows, dark chocolate, red wine and a gallon of drinking water. We intend to make 'smores without the Graham crackers. My wife doesn't eat wheat products, and the rest of us care mostly about the other two-thirds of the traditional 'smores ingredients. I later learn from my son that I have failed because I bought dark chocolate instead of milk chocolate.

At the beach we find a rosy sunset awaiting us. Not only that, a kind careless person has left a smoldering log partially covered with sand. We brush the sand away and fan the fire back to life. The log begins to glow. We find long slim twigs for roasting marshmallows. My son complains the fire isn't flaming up enough and wants to add newspaper. We convince him that the glowing embers are just right for our purposes. I demonstrate by rotating a bulb of soft puffy sugar over the ember until the sweetness is cooked to a golden hue. I lay the warm confection on a slab of dark chocolate and then, on a whim, I give it to my wife. She accepts it gratefully, honored to be the recipient of our first 'smore on the Oregon coast.

We make several more, and the adults chase them down with a very tasty French syrah that was on sale for $8.99 at the market. The rosy orb is sinking by this time and we realize how far we have come from our normal Friday evening routine. We are not absorbed in our respective hobbies and obligations, as we would be if we were home. Instead, the family is huddled together on a beach, in Oregon, with a sunset and a fire and a roaring surf.

We have truly gotten away for the weekend.

Saturday. A walk on the gray beach. Breakfast at the Pig N Pancake. Reading and writing back in the room. I begin this journal. My daughter writes her own version. We drive south to Manzanita, Nehalum and Wheeler. The landscape is increasingly more rural. Manzanita is small, eclectic, charming. We visit the donut shop, and collect firewood from the beach for our evening fire. On the way back north we stop at Oswald Beach State Park and hike a mile down the gently sloping trail to the ocean. Many surfers are there, with dogs. It is a small beach with a rocky shore, perfect as a hiking and picnic destination. Later we walk through the campground to see what the sites are like; it's clearly a surfer hangout, which means loud at night, I imagine. As we pass through the parking lot, young men are unloading surfing gear and beer. Oh, and maybe a cooking utensil or two.

Back in Cannon Beach we rest a while and then drive toward Seaside to play mini-golf and ride go-carts. It was a deal we had made with our kids: if you go for walks and sightseeing with us, we'll take you go-carting. I need cash so I walk next door to a smoky bar to use the ATM. Several men are drinking away the afternoon, watching golf on television and chatting up the barmaid. I get cash and leave. The mini-golf course is a sad homemade imitation of the fancy courses found at the plusher resorts. The go-carts are a bit more exciting. My daughter is thrilled riding next to me as we try to catch up with my son, zipping around corners at stomach-swishing speeds. The top speed is really only about twelve miles per hour, but the cars are low to the ground so they feel faster.

After an uneventful dinner we retire once again to our beach for a fire and a sunset, right on cue. The 'smores are good but the fire is smoky and we all stink after a while.

In the evening, my daughter and I read our stories to the family. Hers is more exciting because she has a refrigerator on fire! There's a simple explanation: the stove is next to the refrigerator. I had boiled water for tea, and from where she sat she saw steam rising from the vicinity of the refrigerator. Therefore, she calmly reported the 'fridge being on fire just before describing what we ate for dinner. Without knowing it, she has given me a lesson in writing.

Sunday. We eat breakfast in the cottage and then walk down the beach to haystack rock. The tide is high so we can't walk out to the rock itself. The top is layered with green vegetation. Seagulls fly around it, and some of them settle among the vegetation, creating a pattern of white dots on a field of green. Down the shore are smaller rocks similar in shape to the big rock. I speculate that we are looking at the remains of a mountain range.

We leave Cannon Beach to begin our journey home. First stop is Fort Clatsop, where Lewis and Clark spent four months during the winter of

1805-1806. The original fort is gone, but a replica has been built using manual tools and methods. Upon reading more about the L&C expedition we solve a great mystery. All over this part of Oregon you see depictions of Lewis and Clark in which one of them, Lewis I suppose, is pointing at something. What is he pointing at? Now we know. The expedition included 24 enlisted men plus 3 sergeants besides Mr. Lewis and Mr. Clark and a few other people. The team did an awful lot of work during their stay in Oregon, preparing for the return trip to St. Louis.

Therefore, we reasoned, when Mr. Lewis was pointing he was giving orders to the men:

"See those trees? Build me a few more dugout canoes."

"Yes, sir."

"See that high bluff? I want a fort right there."

"Yes, sir."

"You, grab those cast iron pots and haul them down to the beach. Start boiling sea water to make salt."

"Yes, sir."

"See those elk and deer? You men round them up for meat and hides."

Whew. After a few months of that I am sure those guys were ready for the relative ease of trekking hundreds of miles back to civilization.

Astoria. A town in transition. It has no doubt seen hard times since the lumber boom ended: poor, depressed, rusted and forgotten. But now, strolling through downtown, we see organic markets and bakeries, music shops, bike shops, art galleries, and all the signs of a flourishing counter-culture movement. The beginnings of gentrification. In three years there will be a Starbucks and a Banana Republic. We walk through a Sunday market and buy food for lunch.

Later we cross the very high bridge from Astoria into Washington. The end of the trip is near. The end of getting away. The drive back through overplanted lumber forests makes me sleepy. My wife drives for a while. We feel relief when we finally pull into our driveway.

We were happy to get away. Now we are happy to be home. I think that was the point of getting away in the first place.

ONE DAY AT THE DEPARTMENT OF HOMELAND HUSBANDS

CAST

Winnie..........deputy assistant director

Monica..........committee member

Tiny............committee member

Peach..........committee member

Luling............committee member

Sheila..........a research subject

Frank...........a research subject

Guard 1...........a male security guard

Guard 2...........a male security guard

Location: Urban 5

Date: June 4, 3013

In a large conference room, four women sit at a table: Winnie, Tiny, Peach and Luling. A wide picture window looks out over an urban landscape of blocks and spires and domes. The women are comfortably dressed, some in flowing garments, others in worn stretchy slacks. The clothing and hair are colorful and whimsical, as are the shoes and accessories.

WINNIE (tapping on the table): The meeting will come to order.

PEACH: But we are not assembled.

TINY: Has anyone heard from Monica?

WINNIE: Monica is always late. We have majority. We can vote.

TINY: Monica has interest in this vote.

WINNIE: Then she should try coming to the meetings on time.

The door to the room slides open. Monica rushes in, looking pink and out of breath.

MONICA: Thank you for waiting.

PEACH: She wasn't going to wait.

WINNIE: That is my prerogative.

MONICA: It's the air transit strike. Of course you've heard.

Monica sits next to Tiny and smiles. She smiles at Peach and Luling across the table. They all smile back.

WINNIE: Of course I *heard*. But I didn't hear from you. Your organizer did not reflect a change of schedule.

MONICA: I didn't have time to update it.

WINNIE: My dear, the transit agency updates everyone's organizer when there's a delay. It's automatic.

MONICA: The transit computers were down. They *couldn't* update.

TINY: It's true, ma'am.

WINNIE (*glaring at Tiny*): Well, since I live right here in Urban 5 I don't take air transit. Therefore I wouldn't know.

Winnie ends the discussion by tapping on the table with a plastic stylus.

WINNIE: Ladies, can we *now* begin the meeting? Is the recorder on?

Peach checks a small device at the end of the table, opposite from Winnie.

PEACH: Yes, ma'am.

WINNIE: Very well. Today is June the 4th in the year three thousand thirteen. The weekly meeting of the Assignments Committee of the Department of Homeland Husbands will now come to order.

Each woman has in front of her a rectangular device for displaying information. The device is about the size of a tablet of paper.

WINNIE: Monica, how many husbands are requested this week?

MONICA: Five hundred and sixty-three.

WINNIE (*raising her eyebrows*): My. There must be some lonely females in our sector.

MONICA: Some of them are requesting husbands for a year.

WINNIE: A year!

LULING: It's not fair. We don't get one for a year and we are on committee.

PEACH: But we get to choose the model we want. That's a far better deal. After all, who would want a husband for a whole year?

LULING: I suppose you're right. After six weeks I'm ready for a new model.

WINNIE: Peach, have you run the inventory report?

PEACH (*reading from her screen*): We have a reduced allocation for our sector. It seems many of the husbands are being diverted to the air system to cover striking workers.

WINNIE: Crap. How long's the strike supposed to last?

PEACH: It goes to world arbitration in two weeks. They are petitioning for new uniforms.

There is a collective groan around the table.

LULING: The module leaders are not going to like this.

WINNIE: Thank you, dear, for stating the obvious.

LULING (*looking around the table*): I think somebody's missing her N-I-3.

WINNIE: It's none of your business.

MONICA: You can have him. The N-I-3 is my least favorite husband model. How much sex can you have in six weeks?

All eyes turned to Winnie.

WINNIE: As much as I want.

PEACH: May I suggest we look at the requests and see what we're lacking.

TINY: Good idea.

They are busy viewing their tablets, tapping their fingers and saying 'Hmm,' and 'Mmm,' and 'No Way.'

LULING: Module 2 doesn't want anything.

MONICA: They've gone a hundred percent Lesbian, so they get first priority at the sperm bank. Makes our job easier.

WINNIE: Can't say I'd want to be in their sandals.

Tiny looks at her coldly.

WINNIE: Oops, that slipped out.

The women are interrupted by a commotion in the hallway. The door slides open and Sheila, wearing a white, zippered body suit, staggers into the meeting room looking very lost.

WINNIE: (*looking annoyed*) Somebody call cryo and tell them they lost a subject. (*pause*) This one looks more lost than usual.

Peach dials a number on her portable communicator.

PEACH (*into phone*): Cryogenic lab? I believe one of your subjects has wandered away again. We're in conference room twenty-four.

SHEILA: Where am I?

WINNIE: Do you have a name?

Tiny goes to the woman and looks at a label on her suit.

TINY: Sheila. Twenty-first century.

WINNIE: Goodness. She's from the neo-dark ages.

TINY (*to the woman*): Are you Sheila?

SHEILA (*nodding*): Where's my husband?

WINNIE: Your husband? What husband?

SHEILA: They woke us up together. He wandered off; he can be so absent-minded, I went looking for him and got lost myself.

MONICA: Do you mean to say your husband from the twenty-first century is walking around here? Lost?

SHEILA: Well, he was a bit lost back then, too. But you learn to work around it, if you know what I mean.

Peach and Luling whisper to each other.

WINNIE: Now, now. Ladies. It's not our concern. Security will collect the subjects in due time.

LULING: But, ma'am, we've never seen a real husband.

WINNIE: You are young, my dear. You need to make friends in the cryo unit and one day you might be invited to observe a research project.

PEACH: You actually saw a real husband? I've always wondered, which model was he like?

MONICA: None. (*All eyes turn to her.*) Well, that's what I've heard.

Sheila has moved closer to the table and listens to the conversation.

SHEILA: What are you talking about? What do you mean by real husband?

WINNIE (*sighing*): My dear, welcome to the year three thousand and thirteen.

Sheila looks like she will faint and grips the table for support. Monica starts to move to catch her.

MONICA: Are you all right?

SHEILA: Thirty-thirteen! That's a thousand years after we were frozen.

TINY: Are you a lab girl?

SHEILA: A what?

WINNIE: There were very few laboratory births at that time.

SHEILA: You mean, was I a test-tube baby? (*laughs*) No one has ever asked me that before.

TINY: These days any woman can fertilize her egg with sperm from a sperm bank and grow her baby in an artificial womb. That's how I was conceived. (*pause*) It's very popular among those who don't care for husbands.

WINNIE (*rolling her eyes*): Here we go again.

TINY: Winnie, you have to admit our models are a poor substitute for the real thing.

SHEILA: Please explain what real thing are you talking about?

The women at the table look at each other.

MONICA (*softly*): A lot has happened in a thousand years. You see, there are very few natural human males left on the planet. Our society today is run entirely by women. It has been for hundreds of years.

SHEILA: What happened to the men?

MONICA: The decline became measurable around the twenty-second century: there was a dramatic drop in male births.

LULING: They don't know exactly why.

TINY: Of course they do: the males became irrelevant to survival.

PEACH: That's what the irrelevists want you to believe. The other theory is gene sabotage.

WINNIE: Pure politics. And everyone knows it.

SHEILA: Gene sabotage?

PEACH: Male scientists invented what was supposed to be the perfect birth control pill, designed to free them of patrimony lawsuits. But it caused a genetic change in women that made males less likely to be born. In a sense, men killed themselves. Which doesn't surprise anyone, of course.

WINNIE: That engineering error was corrected. It's not the cause.

PEACH: The men covered up their mistakes for years. By the time the truth got out, decades had gone by and the trend had already begun. Girls, girls everywhere.

TINY: But you can't deny the irrelevancy argument. By the year twenty-two-fifty men were simply not necessary for survival. In fact, they hindered it by refusing the give up on fossil fuels.

SHEILA: Wait, I'm not awake yet. A thousand years is a long time to go without Starbucks.

MONICA: Without what?

SHEILA: Wow. This really is the future. Wait. You said there are very few *natural* males. Then what kind of males do you have?

MONICA: We breed them.

SHEILA: You breed them!?

LULING: We had to. There was not enough sperm for reproduction, so a famous scientist named Gladys invented syntho sperm. Then she figured out how to create hybrids in order to breed specific qualities in men. At first the models were all called Gladys. But now they go by their model names.

MONICA: The X-H-9 is my favorite. They are bred for creativity and can have long interesting conversations.

WINNIE (*pretending to yawn*): Wake me up when he's gone, please. Try the N-I-3 and you'll see how creative *they* can be.

TINY: Like you really need some man exploring your plumbing night and day.

WINNIE: How would you know?

SHEILA: Do you mean that each husband does one thing?

PEACH: Like cooking.

LULING: Or caring for children.

MONICA: Or handywork around your unit.

WINNIE: Or...

OTHERS (*unison*): We know.

SHEILA: But, my husband did all of those things.

There is sudden silence in the room. Winnie jumps up.

WINNIE: I'd better help find him.

Peach and Luling get up quickly.

PEACH and LULING (*in unison*): I'll go with you.

They pause and regard each other with mistrust. Then they run after Winnie.

SHEILA: Where are they going?

TINY: To find your husband.

SHEILA: What will they do when they find him?

TINY: They will fight over him and the winner will take him home and make him a slave.

SHEILA (*laughing*): I wish them luck. I couldn't do that in twenty years of marriage.

Sheila goes to the window.

SHEILA: What city is this? What country are we in? Everything looks so different.

MONICA: This module is called Urban 5. It contains the remnants of Washington, D.C.

SHEILA: The remnants?

MONICA: In the twenty-third century the city flooded so they moved all of the government functions to the middle of the country. This used to be Kansas.

SHEILA: This is giving me a headache. Washington, D.C., is underwater?

MONICA: There is a natural fall line just west of where D.C. was. When the oceans rose the water returned to its original point.

SHEILA: But, millions of people must have lost their homes and perished.

TINY: Once we got the men out of power we were able to prepare for climate change. By that point anybody with two peas for a brain knew it was coming, but men were still in denial.

MONICA: All of the coastal populations were moved to the center of the country. A new government was established, along with a new legislative body called the Supreme Council. All of the state and city governments were abolished and replaced by modules with a leader and a governing board. All of the resources are shared globally. Of course, it's not perfect. We still have labor strikes and other disruptions.

SHEILA: But planned societies like that were attempted in the past. They never worked.

TINY: Because men were in charge. They couldn't share; they could only compete and invade each other's countries for resources.

SHEILA: But there were women like that, too.

TINY: They imitated men as a survival technique. You couldn't blame them for trying, but it was not their nature.

SHEILA: This is a whole new world. I can't even comprehend it.

MONICA: That's why Module 13 was created. It's for people who don't integrate successfully. Even women are occasionally born with a mutated gene that makes them unfit for module living, which depends on sharing.

TINY: If you have any male tendencies you can't share, you only compete. And when you don't win you start wars. Sometimes they start wars for no reason at all.

SHEILA: Where is Module 13?

MONICA: Do you remember the area known as Detroit?

SHEILA: Michigan? Of course.

MONICA: As you know, it was once a manufacturing center, but long after the personal transportation industry disappeared...

TINY: ...which by the way coincided with men disappearing...

MONICA: ...the Supreme Council made it into a colony for misfits and rejects, and research subjects like yourself. You can take a tour of some of the ancient factories, which were preserved as part of the Male History Tour. You get a glimpse of how society was when men were in charge. They even have a fully preserved section of a football stadium with corporate suites and high-definition T.V. screens.

TINY: Perhaps you can clear up something for me, why would you want a T.V. screen when you have the actual game being played right in front of you.

SHEILA: Some things were mysteries back then, too.

Tiny looks at Monica.

TINY: You realize, of course, Sheila will have to go to Module 13.

MONICA: Seems a shame. I feel she could integrate with a little training.

SHEILA: I don't want to live with the misfits and rejects.

MONICA: It's the law.

SHEILA: Maybe I could hide somewhere with my husband.

MONICA: You can't hide anywhere. The only solution is to petition the Council for an exception to policy.

SHEILA: Will you help me? Please?

Monica looks at Tiny and then back to Sheila.

MONICA: Are you willing to share your husband?

While Sheila, Monica and Tiny are talking, a man knocks and enters the room wearing an armband with the word 'Security' spelled on it.

GUARD 1: I came to retrieve the missing subject.

MONICA: What does the subject look like?

GUARD 1: A male, about six feet tall, dark hair, blue eyes, confused.

SHEILA: That would be Frank.

MONICA (*sigh*): Sounds like a dream husband.

TINY: We will contact you if he shows up.

GUARD 1: I will keep looking. You can call me on my communicator, 1-2-5-0.

TINY: Thank you.

GUARD 1: If I don't answer you can leave a message.

TINY: Thank you.

GUARD 1: Or you can call the dispatcher at 1-3-5-4.

TINY: Thank you.

The guard leaves.

SHEILA: That would be one of your, um, models?

MONICA: He's a T-L-2, bred for security duties. They can watch television and walk around with a flashlight. You can send them on missions but only one mission at a time.

SHEILA: But why didn't he suspect that I am also a subject? I mean, this suit is a dead give-away.

MONICA: He was instructed to look for a man. That's how T-L-2s are, they don't generalize.

SHEILA: Wow. You mean you tell them to do something and they don't forget? What a concept. When I send my husband to the store to get milk he comes back with everything but milk.

MONICA: That's so adorable.

TINY: How sweet. I could almost tolerate a man like that. He would have depth.

SHEILA: Are you kidding? It's maddening. I can see the benefits of your system.

MONICA: Some of us dream of the old days, when men were men and robots were in movies.

SHEILA: I always fantasized about having a husband who did what you told him to do, and only what you told him to do, and never forgot anything.

TINY: You would love today's husbands. They do exactly what you tell them, no more, no less, they don't argue, they don't complain.

MONICA: And they don't laugh. You can't tell them a joke. Although the X-H-9 will pretend to laugh if he figures out that you just told a joke. You have to say something like, 'get it?' at the end.

They are interrupted by a noise at the doorway as Winnie and the others return with a man.

SHEILA (*jumping up from her chair*): Frank! Are you all right?

FRANK: I'm fine honey. How about you?

They hug and kiss. The other women stare.

PEACH: He's so... riveting.

LULING: They don't make them like that anymore.

SHEILA: These nice people have been taking care of me. What have you been doing?

FRANK: I went down a hallway to look for a bathroom and I found a large room that's sort of like a library but it doesn't have any books. Instead it has these nice flat panels that you read from. They're very cool. I want to show them to you.

SHEILA: Frank, how could it be a library if there were no books.

WINNIE: Paper's too expensive, and book-making requires too much energy. We stopped making books centuries ago.

SHEILA: But don't you miss books?

WINNIE: We have panels and tablets, and we have almost one hundred percent literacy. Everybody reads, even the misfits.

SHEILA: Frank, do you know what century we're in? It's thirty-thirteen, a thousand years after we were frozen.

FRANK: A thousand years! That's amazing. I wonder if Hillary Clinton is still president.

MONICA: Winnie, I'm going to petition the Council to keep Frank and Sheila out of Module 13. I believe they can integrate into society, with my help.

WINNIE: Who's going to host them?

MONICA: I will.

WINNIE: I'm sure you don't have the space, my dear. I will host the male subject, and you host the woman.

MONICA: Oh will you? How considerate. But I think we'll manage.

FRANK (*to Sheila*): Dear, what are they talking about?

SHEILA (*to the others*): We would like to stay together and take Monica up on her generous offer.

MONICA: There, it's all settled.

WINNIE: Not quite. You still need Council's approval. Therefore, I can host them right here in Urban 5 until we get the Council decision.

FRANK: Now listen here, folks. What's all this about hosting and councils and urban something or other? I don't like being the subject of someone's conversation without knowing what they're talking about.

The other women step back, amazed.

PEACH: He asserts himself.

LULING: He demands explanations.

WINNIE (*smiling sweetly*): Perhaps I could borrow him for just a little while?

SHEILA: This is my husband you're talking about.

LULING: Okay, when you're done can I try him?

SHEILA: I'm not going to be done. Marriage is forever.

FRANK: Even a thousand years?

SHEILA: Yes, dear. Even a thousand years. The words were 'till *death* do us part.' Being frozen doesn't count.

The door opens and two guards enter.

I am looking for the male subject, said Guard 1.

I am looking for the male subject, said Guard 2.

WINNIE: Are you sure you are both looking for the male subject?

GUARDS (*in unison*): Yes, ma'am.

WINNIE: Sometimes I think we could replace a few more humans around here. What are your instructions?

GUARDS (*in unison*): Male, six feet tall, dark hair, blue eyes, confused.

FRANK: Confused? They must be talking about someone else.

SHEILA: Now, now, dear. You have, on occasion, forgotten where you were or what you were doing.

FRANK: I always know what I'm doing because I'm doing it. I can't help it if other people don't know.

Monica's eyes flutters and she places a hand on her chest.

MONICA: I love the way he argues with her.

PEACH: I've never seen that in a husband.

LULING: Why can't they make a model like that?

WINNIE: Good husbands only come naturally.

SHEILA (*to Frank*): Do you remember that time in Seattle when you were lost in the library?

FRANK: I was looking for a book.

SHEILA: Phooey. You were as lost as a five-year-old. (*to the other women*) The trouble with real husbands is that they won't admit when they need help.

PEACH: I know. It's so charming. Can I rent him from you?

SHEILA: He's not for rent.

The guards move forward and stand on either side of Frank.

GUARD 1: We must escort the subject.

SHEILA: Hey, get your greasy robot hands off my husband.

GUARD 2 (*looking at his hand*): I do not see any grease.

MONICA: We must petition the Council immediately on their behalf. I will take responsibility for the subjects.

LULING: Why does she get the subjects?

SHEILA: Frank. Are we going to be happy here? It's a very different world than the one we left. Washington, D.C., is underwater; everybody lives in Kansas; they have robot husbands, and no Starbucks.

FRANK: I knew *that* wouldn't last.

SHEILA: Oh, and Frank, society is ruled entirely by women.

FRANK: That does it, we're leaving.

SHEILA: We can't, Frank. They can't refreeze us. We're stuck in the future.

FRANK: But I want the good ol' days when men were men and women were barefoot and pregnant.

The other women laugh.

TINY: He's so comical. I could start liking men if I had a real husband.

SHEILA: Comical? That's Frank at his anti-feminist best.

LULING: What was that word? Fem- what?

WINNIE: Feminist. It's from the old days when women had to assert themselves. Once we became the dominant sex the word fell into disuse.

Winnie turns to the Guards.

WINNIE: Guards. Your new instructions are to return to the laboratory and tell them that Winniford Petal is interviewing the subjects.

GUARDS (*unison*): Yes, ma'am.

They leave the room.

SHEILA: Just like that, eh? (*snaps her fingers*) Maybe the future isn't so bad after all.

TINY: It's boring. That's why I prefer the company of women. (*She puts her arm around Sheila.*) You, for example, are a fascinating creature.

SHEILA: You wouldn't like me, I'm a bitch. That's what got us frozen in the first place.

MONICA: Why *did* you do it? Volunteer for cryo, I mean?

SHEILA (*softly*): We had a daughter, a college student. She died in a car crash. We couldn't bear to go on living without her. We heard about a new company that was looking for volunteers to be frozen.

FRANK: They paid us a million dollars each, which has earned interest in an account ever since. We're gazillionaires.

SHEILA: It wasn't about the money. You know how they say time heals all wounds? I thought if we could go away for a long time, a really long time, we would forget about our daughter. But it didn't work. I still remember her like it was yesterday. I still miss her.

TINY: Your mistake was in trying to forget. You never forget a lost love. You learn to live with her memory, and you are grateful for that.

Sheila cries. Frank puts his arm around her.

FRANK (*to Tiny*): You said that very well. Thank you.

All of the other women sniffle and dab their eyes with cloth. Winnie returns to her place at the head of the table and taps her stylus.

WINNIE (*with broken voice*): I hereby adjourn the meeting. We're not getting anything done anyway.

LULING: But, the husband assignments.

WINNIE: Inventory is low anyway because of the transit strike.

PEACH: What about us? I see there's a D-B-8 available. I want him to cook a nice meal for me so I feel better.

LULING: And I want the MOM-2 to watch my kids.

WINNIE: I need my N-I-3.

MONICA: And I want Sheila and Frank to come to my unit to stay.

WINNIE: Oh, all right. I'll petition the Council.

Everyone leaves except Monica, Sheila and Frank.

MONICA: I have a small unit, but I think we'll fit.

SHEILA: We'll be fine. Us women are good at sharing, aren't we?

As they leave, Frank gives a thumbs up with a grin on his face.

THE END

THE PRICE IS WRONG

CAST

Retired Film Maker

Internet Millionaire

The set is a single park bench on an otherwise empty stage.

Scene 1

Film Maker strolls out to the bench from the left, carrying a folded newspaper under his arm. He also carries a small bundle wrapped in a paper towel.

After sweeping off the left end of the bench with the folded newspaper, he sits and spreads the newspaper on his lap. Then he opens the bundle, which contains a nectarine and a sharp knife. He reads the paper while cutting a slice from the fruit. He lifts it to his mouth and eats. He smiles and looks at his surroundings with satisfaction.

Millionaire enters from the right, with a cell phone to his ear.

Millionaire (*into phone*): Ask him to meet me at my usual place in Chicago. Tell him eleven thirty. I'll be there at noon. Yes... that's what I said... noon. I want him to get restless.

Film Maker looks up, annoyed.

Millionaire: No way he's buying lunch. It's my meeting, I'll buy lunch. He just wants to put me on the defensive. I know his type, a real snake oil salesman.

While Millionaire talks, Film Maker looks from his newspaper to the man several times, clearly growing more irritated.

Millionaire: Later, dude. *He closes his phone with a loud clap and puts it away.*

Millionaire stands near the bench and takes in the scenery appreciatively.

Millionaire: What a nice place! (*He looks beyond the bench, to the rear.*) Right on the water. Look how blue it is today. (*He looks forward of the bench, to their front.*) And this park... it's so green. And this is all right in town! It's perfect.

Film Maker rattles his paper and looks down at it. He quietly eats the fruit.

Millionaire *points to the other end of the bench*: May I?

Film Maker *shrugs.* I suspect you are going to regardless.

Millionaire *continues to gaze admiringly as he takes a seat.* What a nice place!

Film Maker *looking bored.* I believe you've made that point.

Millionaire *looks at Film Maker.* You live around here?

Film Maker: You might say I'm local. *Does not look up from paper. Cuts another slice of nectarine.*

Millionaire: I'm thinking of moving here. Just look at these houses, will you? *His gaze is directed in front of them.*

Film Maker: I've seen them.

Millionaire: They must be seventy or eighty years old. Or else replicas.

Film Maker: All originals.

Millionaire: You don't say. They're huge. And look at the details. You know they don't make them like that anymore.

Film Maker *looks up.* That's quite true.

Millionaire: I'm thinking about buying one of these babies. Would make a nice city house for the wife and kids while I'm traveling on business.

Film Maker: Good luck.

Millionaire: What do you mean?

Film Maker: I don't believe any of them are on the market.

Millionaire: Ha. I've heard that before. Fact is, everything's on the market, for a price.

Film Maker: Like I said, good luck finding a seller.

Millionaire *points:* Take that one. Big porch on three sides, and those high windows, and that enormous willow tree. Must be ancient.

Film Maker: It is.

Millionaire: And that rose garden. My wife loves roses.

Film Maker: You don't say. How unique.

Millionaire: What do you think a house like that would go for?

Film Maker: It wouldn't go for anything. It's not for sale.

Millionaire: Nonsense. It's real estate. It has a price.

Film Maker: It happens to be my house, and it has no price because it's not for sale.

Millionaire *looks at Film Maker with admiration.* That's your house?!

Film Maker: Has been for quite a few years.

Millionaire: What's it made of?

Film Maker: Cypress, heart pine, spruce, cherry. Built to last.

Millionaire: Been renovated?

Film Maker *wearily:* New plumbing and electric. Now if you will excuse me, I have some reading to catch up on.

Millionaire: I'll give you a million and a half for it.

Film Maker: That won't even buy the front yard.

Millionaire: Two point three.

Film Maker: Maybe the front yard and part of the back yard. Sir, perhaps you don't appreciate the rarity of historic waterfront homes in one of the nicest neighborhoods on all of Lake Michigan. And trust me, there are a lot of nice neighborhoods on Lake Michigan.

Millionaire: I know, I know. My wife wants a house on the lake. Just like yours. She even described it to me.

Film Maker: Like I said, good luck finding some one who'll sell. These houses are worth more than money.

Millionaire: Nothing's worth more than money.

Film Maker: Except these houses, and a few other very precious things.

Millionaire: You obviously underestimate my net worth.

Film Maker: I've not given it any thought.

Millionaire: For example, you probably don't know that I just sold my Internet advertising company for two hundred and fifty million dollars.

Film Maker: And what does that do for mankind?

Millionaire: It gives me enough money to buy all of these houses if I wish.

Film Maker: Ah, the brimming over-confidence of the newly rich. How tragic and sad and empty. But you're forgetting one very important factor in any potential sale: there needs to be a seller. And you won't find one here. And you certainly won't find one sitting on this bench.

Millionaire: Is that so? Tell me, just how did you manage to land one of these historic houses that no one wants to sell at any price?

Film Maker: I lucked into it.

Millionaire: Let me guess: you're a lawyer. Lawyers are always finding out deals before anybody else.

Film Maker: Nope.

Millionaire: A banker. Bankers hear about good deals every day.

Film Maker: Hardly.

Millionaire: Manufacturing.

Film Maker: Hmm. My detractors have accused me of that.

Millionaire: I knew it. Old manufacturing money. Cars? Appliances? Soap?

Film Maker: Try movies. That no one watches.

Millionaire: Movies? You're a studio owner?

Film Maker: Do I look like an empty-headed moron?

Millionaire: Then what?

Film Maker: Writer and director.

Millionaire: Wow. I've never met a real live film director.

Film Maker: I don't know about the live part.

Millionaire: What movies have you made?

Film Maker: Nothing you've ever heard of.

Millionaire: C'mon. My wife and I watch movies.

Film Maker: How about Rose At Twilight.

Millionaire: Don't recall that one.

Film Maker: Death At Pike Station.

Millionaire shakes his head.

Film Maker: Summer At Blake Island.

Millionaire *snaps his fingers.* Wasn't that an HBO special?

Film Maker: If it was, no one told me about it.

Millionaire: What's your latest movie? Must be in theaters everywhere, right?

Film Maker: My movies have never been in theaters everywhere.

Millionaire: How can that be? You made enough money to buy a house that supposedly no one wants to sell.

Film Maker: I said I lucked into it. My business partner left it to me in his will.

Millionaire *impressed*: Very smooth. Inheritance action. I like it.

Film Maker: There was nothing smooth about it. He was my best friend and collaborator for thirty years and I would gladly give up this house to have him back. I don't think you understand how to interpret the world in any other way than through gold-rimmed glasses. Hey, I kind of like that. Gold-rimmed glasses. You know, instead of rose-colored glasses.

Millionaire: Yeah, I get it. But what you don't get is that money is the common denominator. Everything can be converted into money.

Film Maker: Not everything.

Millionaire: It's just a question of how much.

Film Maker finishes his fruit and wipes the knife with the paper towel. Then he wraps the pit and the knife in the paper towel and places the bundle on the bench next to him.

Millionaire: You come out here all the time?

Film Maker: Everyday.

Millionaire: Thinking about your next movie?

Film Maker: I'm retired.

Millionaire: Why retire? Don't you want to make more movies?

Film Maker: I know when to stop.

Millionaire: Who watches your movies?

Film Maker *shrugs:* Perhaps a few film students now and then.

Millionaire: So you didn't make money from your movies. Then why did you keep making them?

Film Maker: Now that would be one of the mysteries of life, wouldn't it. I don't think your type would understand.

Millionaire: Ah. It was the women. I heard that Alfred Hitchcock slept with all of his leading ladies.

Film Maker: He was a crass womanizer.

Millionaire: But he made money, and he got the girls.

Film Maker: It was never my wish to be polluted with money and casual sex.

Millionaire: I see. You were a critical and artistic success!

Film Maker: The critics were not overly fond of my films, except for a few who saw what I was trying to do. But most of them wouldn't know art if you hit them over the head with it.

Millionaire: Let me tell you about my Internet advertising business.

Film Maker: Do I have a choice?

Millionaire: It gives businesses a way to reach specific segments of the marketplace.

Film Maker: You mean specific segments of people who happen to be spending all of their time on computers.

Millionaire *excited:* Yes, yes. We reach leading edge consumers.

Film Maker: Oh brother. In that case I want to be on the trailing edge. So far behind that I'm off the edge.

Millionaire: Hey, you're not getting my point. With a proper marketing investment you could sell your movies on DVD to people all over the world who like your kind of work.

Film Maker *sighs:* There are damned few of them. Besides, I don't even own the rights. Talk to the studio.

Millionaire: But if you put up the money they would jump on it, and you can negotiate a share of the proceeds.

Film Maker: I don't have that kind of money anyway.

Millionaire *slowly turns his head to look in front of them, at the house:* Are you sure?

Film Maker *follows his gaze and understands:* It's not for sale.

Millionaire: Six million.

Film Maker: At any price.

Millionaire: Eight point five.

Film Maker: It's worth more than money.

Millionaire: You said that.

Film Maker: But you weren't listening.

Millionaire: This isn't about money. This is about your legacy as a filmmaker. Don't you want to be a legend?

Film Maker: That's for insecure idiots. I know who I am and I know what I've done. My films are available in a few film school libraries if anyone wants to watch them.

Millionaire: You can do better than that. A smart distributor could get your films in every video rental store in the country.

Film Maker: Who cares?

Millionaire: But don't you want to be rewarded for your work?

Film Maker: I was rewarded. I made the movies. The rest is somebody else's job.

Film Maker *gathers his things:* I'm afraid you've ruined my morning. *He puts the folded paper under his arm and picks up the bundle containing the knife and pit with his left hand. The blade of the knife protrudes from his grip.*

Millionaire *gets up quickly:* Ten million dollars. Cash. No inspection, no contingencies. How can you say no to that?

Film Maker: It's easy. *No.*

Millionaire: Listen. I've worked ninety-hour weeks for as long as I can remember to make my fortune. It's a grind. Don't tell me money isn't worth anything. My wife hates me. My kids don't know me. I have to get this house to save my marriage.

Film Maker: Get hold of yourself, man.

Millionaire: I need your house.

Film Maker: It's not for sale.

Film Maker stands and tries to walk away, still holding the knife with the blade pointing out.

Millionaire *blocks his way:* Nobody just walks away from easy money like that.

Film Maker: It would not be easy money. I would have to give up something that's worth everything for something that's worth nothing.

Millionaire: Money is worth nothing to you?

Film Maker: It is not worth anything to anybody. Haven't you seen that bumper sticker: 'the good things in life are not things' ?

Millionaire: Try telling that to my wife.

Film Maker: Don't blame it on her. She's probably as bored as you are. When was the last time you had a decent conversation with your wife?

Millionaire: That's a good idea. I'd like to have that conversation in your kitchen, after it becomes our kitchen.

Film Maker: Don't hold your breath. *Steps around Millionaire and starts to walk away.*

Millionaire: My final offer: twelve million. Can you afford to say no to that?

Film Maker *pauses:* Did you say twelve million?

Millionaire: Twelve million dollars.

Film Maker: That is a lot of money.

Millionaire *folds his arms:* It's finally sinking in.

Film Maker *looks at Millionaire, appears to be thinking:* Can we meet here tomorrow?

Millionaire: Of course we can.

Scene 2

Millionaire is waiting at the bench, cell phone to ear. Film Maker walks in from left.

Millionaire *into phone*: What do you mean?

Film Maker takes a seat. Millionaire turns away slightly.

Millionaire: What's that supposed to mean? I thought I explained that? ... Look I have a meeting. Can I call you later?

Millionaire closes phone slowly.

Film Maker *is chipper:* You know, I'm glad I ran into you yesterday. I needed someone like you to come along and talk some sense into me.

Millionaire: What are you saying?

Film Maker: I'm frankly embarrassed to admit that you were right. Even I have a price for things I thought were priceless. Twelve million dollars is too much to turn down for that house. At first I was ashamed, but then I thought of what I could do with that money. I have grandchildren you know.

Millionaire *unsmiling:* Unfortunately, twelve million is too much to pay for that house.

Film Maker: What?

Millionaire: It's way over market price.

Film Maker: But you offered twelve million.

Millionaire: That was yesterday, and you didn't take it.

Film Maker: But today I'm willing to sell.

Millionaire: Ah, now we have a seller but no buyer.

Film Maker: What kind of a con is this?

Millionaire: A con? Paying market price for a house is not a con, my friend. It's a fair transaction.

Film Maker: I suppose you have researched the market price.

Millionaire: Four point two million.

Film Maker: Nonsense. It's historic. I could sell it on eBay for eight million.

Millionaire: That's still a lot less than twelve million.

Film Maker: Why the change? What's happened?

Millionaire *looks at his cell phone:* My wife wants a divorce.

Film Maker *looks down:* Oh. Sorry to hear that.

Millionaire: She's had enough. The travel, the long hours. Raising the kids by herself. I can't say I blame her.

Film Maker: Buy the house! That'll cheer her up.

Millionaire: She won't even look at it.

Film Maker: Send her a picture. She'll fall in love with it.

Millionaire: I tried. She won't read my emails.

Film Maker *snaps his fingers:* Say, how about this: buy the house and tell her you'll quit your job. She gets the house of her dreams, and her husband back.

Millionaire *shakes his head:* It's too late. We've had too many fights, too many bad words. It can't work.

Film Maker: Hey what happened to all that confidence I saw yesterday? You were overflowing with it: a master of the universe, a man in charge. Now you look like a puppy left out in the rain.

Millionaire: You don't know what it's like.

Film Maker: Oh I do know. You can't be in the movie business for thirty years without taking a few scrapes in the romance department.

Millionaire: Wait a minute, I thought you didn't sleep with your actresses.

Film Maker: I said I didn't go for casual sex. My true love was a woman I spent ten years with but was too cowardly to marry. We had a daughter who is now grown up and won't speak to me. She won't even give me her address so I can send birthday presents to my grandchildren.

Millionaire: You should reach out to them.

Film Maker: Look who's talking. Buy my house and I will reach out to them, with money. It's the universal language.

Millionaire: That's not what you said yesterday. What have I created?

Film Maker: I know. I know. A change has come over me. I've been hiding away in that house all these years. Hiding from society, from my family. It's become a crutch, an escape. I need to break out of this... this stupor that I've been in. I need to get a life.

Millionaire: Glad to have helped. I'll give you three point five for the house.

Film Maker: But you said the market price was four point two million!

Millionaire: You don't get rich paying market price my friend.

Film Maker: What would you do with the house if I sold it?

Millionaire: Paint it a new color and resell it in four months for twice as much.

Film Maker: You big money guys are all alike. Reminds me of people who invest in movies. They have no soul, no character.

Millionaire *quietly*: You misunderstand me. I'm deliberately offering you a bad deal because I don't believe you should sell the house. You see, it is worth more than money, in a way. You couldn't build that house today at any price. You can't buy the materials. You can't find the craftsmen who know how to do that kind of detail work. The window casings alone are priceless. I walked by it last night.

Film Maker: You did?

Millionaire: Like you said, I did my homework. And my recommendation is, don't sell.

Film Maker: But I want to sell.

Millionaire: But you are attached to that house. It's part of you. And your favorite collaborator lived there. It's part of that person, too.

Film Maker: But it's time to move on. I'm not getting any younger, in case you haven't noticed. I don't want to spend my last years rocking on that porch, waiting for the inevitable.

Millionaire: Good for you. This makes me feel like I've done something useful for society.

Film Maker: Tell you what, I'll take market price. Four point two million and not a dollar less.

Millionaire: You've come a long way from twelve million.

Film Maker: I can do a lot with four million. I can put my grandchildren through college. Besides, this isn't about my needs. This is about your family. Buy that house. Show your wife you have some values. She'll come back to you. As long as you promise to stay home. Hey, with your money you could open a little office. See that coffee shop down the block? There's a space for rent right above it.

Millionaire follows Film Maker's gaze away off to the left. Millionaire looks dreamy, contemplating.

Millionaire: You may have something there. Let's meet tomorrow and I'll give you my answer.

Film Maker: Deal.

They shake hands.

Scene 3

The bench sits empty. The sound of wind is heard. Leaves rustle. Birds twitter.

A person wearing a PARK STAFF t-shirt enters from right with a broom and a long-handled dust pan, the kind park employees use so they can scoop up trash without having to bend over. The person sweeps around the bench and brushes off a few leaves and twigs from the seat, and then scoops the debris into the dust pan.

The person moves off to the left. The bench sits empty on the stage. The lights dim, then darkness.

THE END

ANALOG MOMENT

rain rain soft as air felt not seen cool warm cool again mist in the harbor or maybe just more rain looks like mist from a distance soaking rain long rain rivers of rain glistening collecting swirling spilling wet: shoulders shoes hands hat ears hair nose wind blurred vision ahead i see her black coat red hair white purse a dream who is she

the ferry she buys coffee i buy coffee i hate coffee i smile no response red hair thick luxurious heavy wet wool sweater white purse large organized crisp smells of wet leather blackberry cell phone ipod working earning living for tomorrow paying bills today in touch always ball and chain no such thing as a labor saving device the boss expects more because you can do more don't get caught without your phone of all the gin joints in all the world she sits across from me i was a non-entity two minutes ago perhaps i still am blending in with the furniture non-threatening just another faceless passenger part of the scenery yep that's me she has a computer slim trim powerful the computer i mean got to stay in touch bits bits bytes bits bytes and more bytes lots of ones and zeros billions upon billions yet where is the communication just keep talking doesn't matter what you say blast 'em until their eyes glaze over then you'll be the boss one day kid take it from me i clawed my way to the top before computers if i had one back then i'd be god now thou art god said the man from mars strangers in a very strange land yeah this is mighty strange god is all of us or god is none of us

rain goes mountains appear if you don't like the weather wait five minutes pink orange white glowing in the west backlit in the east red sky green harbor white boats peaks valleys another morning thank you peace she reads email i read my book heinlein the man from mars would know what to do never in a hurry waiting is a concept waiting is waiting is this is living this is god right now spring on the island a smudge of light green like a painting almost too good to be real rainier majestic imagine the first people it must have been a marvel to them it must have been god still is waiting is timeless they had all the time we have no time sliced and diced and wrapped and stacked hogs union stockyards chicago big names of the gilded age: armour pullman men of steel women harder than steel molten iron poured formed glazed seattle bombers b-17s all lined up heros zeros aces bigger than life lower than life

but

you could get away with murder none of this media crap too much information too little information back then a man could do what he needed to do no tattletales and whistleblowers and blogging fruitcakes and youtube and every other person a journalist from hell god is everywhere or god is nowhere gilded men are on the run

she crosses her legs

what is living when does it start when does it stop religion man- made choose one any one take door number two sure path to salvation culture community tradition generations sons and fathers daughters and mothers rituals provide comfort and continuity we bond in ritual what doesn't kill you makes you stronger what is her religion red hair irish catholic let's reduce her to a stereotype so much easier to deal with molly bloom now there's an irish catholic if i ever saw one "yes and his heart was going like mad and yes i said yes i will yes" wow kind of takes your breath away that must be living what do we call this that we do now what does she do for kicks when she's not emailing ipodding blackberrying phoning communicating when she's off line when she's analog when she's face to face eye to eye lips to lips dinner candles music conversation about flowers fragrant sushi sake texture taste wood cloth glass sensations she's living then coming out of the digital world going analog warm humming heart beating eyes batting love smiles kisses and more she's human again for the moment when does it happen with whom

with a chirp and a sigh her computer goes away into the big white bag i sense my time is running out what a coward i am a life of missed opportunities why break my streak now what would the men of steel do the industrialists built this country and made the rules they are god or no one is god big money oodles of money house in the city house in the country houses of mirth money makes the world go 'round modern millionaires have no taste the gilded man had a box at the opera today's man has a box at the stadium drinking bad beer the old-timers had an eye for quality and style today's millionaires buy bigger and more of it forty-inch hdtv with nothing to watch but commercials or worse the barons robbed you in style the titans of today rob you until they get caught trading inside outside the law backdating options cooking the books like burnt chicken on fourth of july

she stands

i wonder if she is married to a big money man or maybe she is a money woman herself some of them ride their own motorcycles and have their own offices at no man's beck and call slim trim powerful her i mean with a toss of those scented locks she steps away a fragrance rattles my insides but wait! an item left on the seat not something that one would toss away not even a millionaire babe or a millionaire's wife a fine pen a writing instrument solid in the hand you would sign important documents with it contracts engines of finance and business nothing happens without a contract and if it's not in the contract it definitely doesn't happen no freebies today ever try to define quality? it was understood once upon a time among the big money men they bought quality and quality was delivered houses cars furniture built to last a long time you could pass them down through the generations along with your culture and your rituals and your prejudices and your greatest fears a package deal handed down to sons and daughters quality was part of the package now it is rare because it's not in the contract sorry ma'am the building code doesn't say to do that so you bought a million-dollar pile of sticks and filled it with crap congratulations you've arrived

i grab the pen and hurry to catch up with her she walks fast a babe with a purpose look out i've seen the type sunlight gleaming buildings fresh air she joins the huddled masses on the deck i approach: your pen? her mask melts away like magic she becomes analog and warm and womanly gracious smiling genuine i am without a doubt the kindest and most thoughtful person in the world she murmurs a gushing word of thanks i ask about the pen it seems fine indeed a gift from her father she says who had received it from his father a treasure an item of quality handed down to be used again because it can be an item still in service so rare so spectacular i wondered what else had been handed down to her kindness common sense

which way are you walking

first avenue

me too

we leave together a moment of quality to be treasured

this is living

this is analog

NOTES

ANGELA. Winner of the 2006 Emerging Writer Award from Humanities Washington, a Seattle-based nonprofit supporter of community arts and literature programs. I adapted the story from a larger serialized work called "Night Watch" that I wrote on my blog. The story is a chronicle of my wife going into labor and giving birth to our second child, assisted by a doula.

CONVALESCENCE. Honorable Mention (second place) in the Richard Hugo House Quarter Genre Competition. Hugo House is a Seattle literary center that serves writers with classes, workshops and the community of other writers. The theme of the contest was "one foot on the floor."

SHOPPING AT MAISON BLANCHE. Appeared in SOUTHERN REVIVAL: Deep Magic For Hurricane Relief, 2005, edited by Tamara Sellman. The characters and setting were inspired by memories of my aunts and grandmother on my mother's side of the family.

"J" Appeared in OBLIQUITY, a collection of speculative fiction from Northwest writers, 2006, Tuesday Night Publishing. It represents my fascination with the Catholic Church and New Orleans, where I grew up.

SEEKING REFUGE AT THE PALM COURT. An essay about New Orleans a year after Hurricane Katrina. I was in town for a book convention and spent an evening checking out the French Quarter.

HOW I'M HANDLING MY MIDLIFE CRISIS. A little humor piece that I wrote for a Seattle newspaper. I was basically in denial about aging.

GETTING AWAY. This little essay is about a family getaway to the Oregon coast.

ONE DAY AT THE DEPARTMENT OF HOMELAND HUSBANDS. This play portrays a theme I've had in mind for years, which is basically that women will eventually rule the universe, or at least the part of it called planet Earth.

THE PRICE IS WRONG. I wrote this on the porch of a house in Door County, Wisconsin, with a beautiful view of Lake Michigan. It's about two men who meet on a park bench.

ANALOG MOMENT. This is the one poem in the collection. It's really a spoken-word performance piece. The characters and setting come from my days of commuting to Seattle by ferry. The format of this poem is intentionally stream of consciousness, let the words associate freely in your head as you read and a picture will emerge.

Notes composed August 4, 2012. Seattle.

www.ingramcontent.com/pod-product-compliance
Lightning Source LLC
Chambersburg PA
CBHW020632130626
46552CB00003B/1187